RUDE AWAKENING

RUDE AWAKENING

A Milt Kovak Mystery

Susan Rogers Cooper

This first world edition published 2009
in Great Britain and in the USA by
SEVERN HOUSE PUBLISHERS LTD of
9–15 High Street, Sutton, Surrey, England, SM1 1DF
Trade paperback edition published
in Great Britain and the USA 2009 by
SEVERN HOUSE PUBLISHERS LTD

British Library Cataloguing in Publication Data

Cooper, Susan Rogers.
  Rude Awakening.
  1. Kovak, Milton (Fictitious character) – Fiction.
  2. Sheriffs – Oklahoma – Fiction. 3. Detective and mystery
  stories.
  I. Title
  813.5'4-dc22

ISBN-13: 978-0-7278-6741-4   (cased)
ISBN-13: 978-1-84751-160-7   (trade paper)

All Severn House titles are printed on acid-free paper.

Typeset by Palimpsest Book Production Ltd.,
Grangemouth, Stirlingshire, Scotland.
Printed and bound in Great Britain by
MPG Books Ltd., Bodmin, Cornwall.

*To intrepid fan and sometime contributor Joe Burkholder
and to Tristan Cooper-Brooks, the new man in my life*

ACKNOWLEDGMENTS

I would like to thank my readers and fellow writers, Jan Grape, Nancy Bell, and Evin Cooper for their insight and courage, and, as always, Vicky Bijur, my friend and agent. I would also like to thank Anna and Amanda from Severn House for their encouragement and insightful editing.

PROLOGUE

EMIL HAWTHORNE

D r Emil Hawthorne woke up in a very bad mood. That he woke up at all was a medical miracle; one of those incidents desperate family members point to in an attempt to delay pulling the plug on a loved one. For Dr Emil Hawthorne had woken up after eight years in a coma. Another unusual thing about Dr Hawthorne was that he awoke with total recall of the accident that had caused the head injury, putting his life on hold for eight years. He was on his way to have a chat with a colleague, and he was traveling at eighty miles per hour in a fifty-five-mile-an-hour zone. He barely saw the large pickup truck perched atop its monster-truck tires as it slammed into him – after he ran the red light.

The good news, I suppose you could say, was that Dr Emil Hawthorne woke at all. The bad news was that he woke up to the fact that his medical license had been revoked and his fully restored, 1963 classic Corvette, that he'd been driving during the accident, had been totaled, long ago having been smashed flat at the junk yard. His penthouse apartment on Chicago's Michigan Avenue had been sold, along with his very small Cézanne, his Shaker sideboard, the antique Oriental rug in his den and anything else of value; all in order to pay for the exorbitant medical bills produced by eight years of a coma. Everything else had been either sold at a garage sale or given to Good Will.

When Dr Emil Hawthorne woke up that morning, he owned exactly nothing; even the gown covering his body belonged to the hospital.

The one thing he did own, as those in his former profession would say, was his anger. The anger that had led him to the high-speed romp that ended in his current situation.

The anger those eight years in a coma could not sway. The anger directed at one person, and one person alone. His betrayer.

Dr Jean MacDonnell.

That had been six months ago – a very long six months. When you have no further to fall, the only option is up, and Dr Emil Hawthorne was able to pull in a few favors still owed, take advantage of a little guilt here and there, gather up sufficient funds to finance his venture. It wasn't a money-making venture, per se. If he saw a profit, then so be it. The venture was, in and of itself, revenge, plain and simple.

Dr Emil Hawthorne was going to get some of his own back, come hell, high water or a hick sheriff – who just happened to be his betrayer's husband.

PART I
REVENGE

ONE

DALTON PETTIGREW

Dalton Pettigrew was in love. It was the first time since Sally Jeffries in the ninth grade, and he'd never gotten up the courage to speak to her, much less to ask her out. But here he was now, in a three-month-old relationship, and with a girl as pretty as a postcard: golden hair, big blue eyes and a smile so sweet it could take your breath away. Her name was Sarah and she lived in Tulsa. She was kind and gentle, a little bit shy, and Dalton knew in his heart that they would be together forever.

All he had to do was to actually meet her.

Dalton knew that people – mainly his boss, Sheriff Milt Kovak – thought of him as kind of stupid, but he wasn't really. Dalton just didn't have a lot of confidence, which is why he asked so many questions. He just wanted to make sure that he had everything absolutely straight in his head before he attempted something. He didn't like making mistakes, and if asking a lot of what people called 'fool questions' kept him from making mistakes, then so be it. 'Better to look a fool than be a fool,' his mama always said. And in Dalton's line of work, a mistake could cost somebody his life. A few years back Dalton had done something that made him a hero in the eyes of the town, and he'd gloried in that – but not for long. As his mama often said, 'The real question is: what have you done lately?' Meaning: Don't rely on the praise of past glories; nobody'll remember them, except for you.

Not being stupid, Dalton hadn't told anyone – not even his mama – about Sarah. He'd told a friend back in the ninth grade about Sally Jeffries, and it had gotten all over school and made him look a fool. 'Better to look a fool than be a fool' always ended with his mama adding, 'But never look a fool if you can help it.' So he emailed Sarah every night, sometimes three or four times if she kept answering him, from the privacy of his bedroom computer. Sometimes they'd IM each other, just like having a phone conversation, except without awkward silences or stuttered words on his part.

But now Sarah wanted to meet him. Wanted him to come to Tulsa. Just the thought made his palms sweat and ears ring. What if she didn't like him? She said she thought he was handsome in his picture, but that only showed his face, with his gray-green eyes, blond hair in standard military cut and lopsided smile with one dimple. He always thought that one dimple and the crooked smile made him look a little stupid, but she had said she thought he looked handsome. But what if she didn't realize he was a 'big old boy'? Maybe she didn't like 'em real tall or real big. Not that Dalton was fat: most of it was muscle, but sometimes that put off some girls. Or so his mama said.

Sarah – what a sweet, old-fashioned name. He thought it went well with her picture. In it, she wore a pale pink sweater set and a strand of pearls, her hair to her shoulders and slightly flipped out at the ends. No piercings, no tattoos. They'd talked about that, and she'd been adamant that it was a sacrilege to deface one's body in such a way. 'Your body is your temple,' she'd written, 'created by God in his image. Would you stick holes in God? Put a picture of a butterfly on God?'

Dalton had agreed with her 100 per cent. He wasn't a particularly religious person, although he went with his mama to the Church of Christ every Sunday. He mostly daydreamed or slept during the sermon, and he hadn't read the Bible since he was a boy. But he agreed that piercing or tattooing one's body was somehow offensive to God.

Dalton very much wanted to meet Sarah, but he wanted that part to be over. He wanted them to just move on to the part where they loved each other and wanted to get married and have babies. At thirty-four, Dalton was definitely ready for that part of his life to begin. He was tired of just being 'Uncle Dalton' to his sister's three kids and his brother's four. He wanted his own. And he wanted Sarah.

In his daydreams, he saw Sarah in their kitchen, all white and yellow, with her in that pink sweater set, feeding their baby at the kitchen table, the baby – a boy, of course – in his high chair, laughing and gurgling as his mama spooned in the food. In his daydreams, Dalton stood watching them, a smile on his face, content with his lot in life. Sometimes he saw the two of them, he and Sarah, at the zoo in Tulsa on a Sunday: Sarah with a little girl in a stroller, he with his son riding on his shoulders. They were laughing and pointing at the animals; the children excited, and he and Sarah looking on with good-humored indulgence.

One of his favorite daydreams was being in Sheriff Kovak's backyard, with the sheriff's young son Johnny Mac teaching Dalton's boy how to throw a ball, and Sarah and Jean talking women's talk, Dalton's baby girl sitting on his lap as he listened to the sheriff talk about this or that as he barbecued steaks for the grown-ups and hot dogs for the kids. This could be Dalton's life.

If he'd just go to Tulsa and meet Sarah.

MILT KOVAK

If somebody ever suggests to you to move to a small town and run for sheriff, shoot 'em. It's not the glory job you might think. I was sitting in my office writing out a report to the county commissioners on why I thought it would be a good thing to have a traffic light on the corner of Mitchem Road and Highway-5. The fact that we've had fourteen accidents there in the past ten years wasn't enough to sway them, since not one was a fatality.

It was three o'clock in the afternoon and it had not been a good day. Hell, it was Friday, and it hadn't been a good *week*. In the wee hours of Monday morning, Dale Davies got his foot stuck in a culvert grate over on Hayes Street and was too drunk to figure out how to get it out and just started screaming. Now, Dale lives on Hayes Street and it woulda been all right if Marlene, Dale's wife, had been the first one to hear him screaming, but that wasn't the case. Four other households on Hayes Street heard him before Marlene – who'd been up late watching Dave Letterman – even woke up. Three of those other households were on to the sheriff's department right away; the fourth, having just moved to Hayes Street from inside the city limits of Longbranch and not remembering they were in the county now, called the police department.

Anthony Dobbins, Prophesy County's first and only African-American deputy, was first on the scene, but then he got into a jurisdictional dispute with Vern Neuman, the police officer on call for the city. Now, Vern's not a card-carrying member of the Ku Klux Klan or anything like that, but he's not what you'd call enlightened either. He made a rude remark to Anthony, who made a rude remark back; all the time both of 'em forgetting poor old Dale Davies, whose foot was still stuck in the culvert grate and was still screaming fit to beat the band. So the three households who'd called the sheriff's department, and the one household who'd called the police department, all hit redial and eventually me and Charlie Smith, the Longbranch Police Chief, had to get out of our separate beds, pull on our separate britches and go the hell down to Hayes Street and figure out the mess.

And that was before Monday had even really begun. Later that afternoon I had a 'shots fired' called in from out in the country and, being March and not hunting season, we had to deal with it. But the country, being big like it is with just some mile markers and a bunch of trees as landmarks, is not a real good description, so we never found the perpetrator, nor did we find anything dead.

Tuesday was just the usual crap. But then Wednesday, Arlene Edgewater called in to say that she'd had a peeping Tom the night before. Now, Arlene is seventy-five if she's a day, and I'm not saying she's not a good-looking woman, even at seventy-five, but we don't get a lot of peeping toms going after the senior set. Which just goes to show what an ageist I am, even in *my* advanced years. Wednesday night, while Dalton Pettigrew was doing his rounds (going by Miz Edgewater's house special because I asked him to), he caught Lon Robert Brown peeping in Miz Edgewater's bedroom window. Dalton called me down to the station to deal with Lon Robert, who's ninety-three. He had figured out some way to get out of his daughter Lois's house, even though she's got keyed deadbolts on every door in the house, due to her daddy's Alzheimer's. I called Lois, who Dalton easily could have called himself, but he didn't, and had a long talk, *again*, with her about having her daddy put in a home. By the time I got back to my house on Mountain Falls Road, all the lights were on and Johnny Mac, my four-year-old son, was sitting in his mama's lap in the living room, running a temperature of 102 point something.

So on Thursday I stayed home in the morning with Johnny Mac and went in after lunch when my wife Jean came home for her turn.

Which gets us back to Friday. Johnny Mac woke up perfectly OK. Jean fixed him oatmeal for breakfast, even though he insisted he wanted McDonald's. So, like an idiot, I promised him McDonald's for lunch. So Jean took him to pre school, and I picked him up at noon, and we met his mama at McDonald's. As anyone with kids knows, McDonald's is *haute cuisine* for the Happy Meal set, and a decent reward for a four-year-old who managed to outsmart a temperature.

So he got four-piece chicken McNuggets with ranch, apple slices with caramel dipping sauce and chocolate milk, all in a Happy Meal with a cheap plastic toy, which is the real reason most kids even want to go to McDonald's. Jean got a salad, and I got a Big Mac and large fries. Jean and I got to talking, not really noticing how many of my fries Johnny Mac was managing to shovel into his mouth, along with his own concoction of ranch dressing mixed with ketchup (if you don't look directly at it, it's not *that* bad). He'd already managed to finish his chicken nuggets, apple dippers and most of his chocolate milk.

There was absolutely no warning. The boy just spewed. Blew chunks everywhere – all over himself, his mama and me. And he just didn't stop. The lady sitting next to us began to dry heave, which got her two-year-old crying, and the manager, Sharon Maggert, who me and my ex-wife

used to double date with back the summer after we graduated high school, came running out, screaming my name
and pointing at the door.

By this time, Johnny Mac had quit spewing, so I picked
him up and rushed toward the door. Unfortunately, I was
holding him around the middle, which I now see might
have been a mistake. As we approached the doors, he projec-
tile vomited, hitting the glass doors, the floor, the life-size
cut-out of Ronald MacDonald standing next to the door and
the booth closest to us.

Sharon didn't even let Jean finish cleaning up, just asked
us to leave and to use the drive-thru from now on. I thought
that was rude, but Jean said just to leave her be, so I did.
We all headed back home for a change of clothes. I left
Johnny Mac and Jean back at the house and headed back
to the station.

And for those of you who might be asking yourselves,
hey, isn't he too old to have a four-year-old son? The answer
is yes, I am. Way too old. I'm now doing something I
shoulda done thirty years ago, i.e., being a daddy. But thirty
years ago it didn't happen. It happened four years ago, and
what's a fella to do? At somewhere around the sixty mark
(and I'm not telling if it was north or south), I met a lady
named Jean, who took a fancy to a paunchy, balding deputy
sheriff, who just happened to have a killer smile and a
sparkle in his blue eyes. That's me, folks. And the rest, as
they say, is history.

So, here it was: three o'clock on a Friday afternoon,
and I was making up statistics on the eminent probability
of a fatality on Mitchem Road and Highway-5, and trying
to get the smell of Johnny Mac's spew out of my nostrils,
when I got an intercom call from Gladys, our civilian
clerk.

'Milt,' she said, with that no-nonsense sound to her voice.
'You need to get out here.'

Hitting the switch to talk, I said, 'I'm busy.'

'Now,' she said, and her tone brooked no argument.
Thinking *she ain't the boss of me* did little to keep me in
my seat. Having been raised by a mama whose 'now' meant

serious business, I was kinda like Pavlov's dog to that word. I went into the large area where Gladys ruled.

Two things caught my eye. The first was Gladys standing behind her counter, arms across her chest, a scowl on her face. The second was what she was scowling at. Namely, my deputy Dalton Pettigrew's mama.

Dalton's mama was five foot nothing, weighed about eighty-five pounds and was wearing a workout suit that appeared to come from the boy's department of J.C. Penney's. The running shoes on her tiny feet lit up when she moved – definitely from the boy's department. She had very short salt-and-pepper hair, glasses and a hawkish nose. And she ruled the roost at her house like nobody's business – and had since Dalton's daddy went out for a pack of cigarettes one night and never came back. 'Course, maybe she ruled the roost before that, too, which may have been *why* Dalton's daddy left. And it looked like she was trying to rule the roost here now, too. The fact that this was definitely, and without question, Gladys's roost didn't seem to impress the lady much.

My cousin Earl, gone now for some twenty-odd years, was a friend of Dalton's daddy. I was in grammar school when they were hanging out, but I remember the elder Pettigrew well. Dalton is definitely a clone of his daddy: big and blond and not very bright; Dalton's daddy should have been a football player but was too clumsy to do much. His name was Peter Pepperidge Pettigrew, known throughout the high school as 'Threepee'. After high school he went away from Longbranch, coming back about a year later with wife, Clovis, and the first of the three Pettigrew children: Hawke, another clone of his daddy. Unfortunately, the middle child was a girl, Mary Ellen, and she, too, took after Threepee. That boy had some serious genes.

Seeing me, Gladys said, 'I've been telling her Dalton doesn't come on duty til Monday!'

'That so?' I said.

'That's what the roster says!' Gladys said, staring daggers at me and shoving the roster under my nose. Seeing as it was a Friday, and Gladys had initiated 'casual Fridays' a couple of years back, she was attired that day in stretch denim pants that covered what my nephew Leonard said was called 'junk in the trunk', which Gladys had a serious amount of, and a long-sleeved denim shirt that Gladys herself had appliquéd with multicolored spring flowers, yellow-and-black bumblebees and pink and purple butterflies. Her champagne blonde hair was curled in a tight new perm and her cheeks were as rosy as Max Factor could make 'em.

I pushed the roster back a bit, so I could see what she was shoving under my nose, and looked. It definitely said Dalton was off today, through the weekend and not on again until Monday morning.

I showed the roster to Clovis Pettigrew. 'That's what it says,' I said.

'Well, that's not what my boy told me!' she said, hands on hips, scowl on face. Actually, I've never seen her face look anything other than how it did now, so maybe it wasn't a scowl, maybe that was just the way her face looked. Or maybe she'd been scowling for so long, the wind changed and she now wore it permanently, just like my mama always warned me.

'He said he was coming in to work this morning?' I asked, picking up real quick like, which is what a duly elected sheriff should do.

'He left yesterday evening, saying he had to work the night shift. Then when he didn't come home this morning like he was supposed to, I got to calling his cell phone. And instead of talking to me, there was a message saying he had to work straight through to Monday. Some undercover thing!' Clovis said.

Uh oh, I thought. We don't do undercover, and even if we did, I'd never use Dalton for such a thing. The boy wouldn't be able to persuade a two-year-old that he was anything other than a cop.

'Ma'am,' I said to Dalton's mama, 'let me look into this and I'll get right back to you. I've got your number and I'll give you a call.'

Arms back across her chest. 'No, I don't think so,

Sheriff,' she said. 'I think I'll just wait here until you produce my son.'

'That'll be kinda hard, Miz Pettigrew,' I said, thinking fast. 'With Dalton being undercover and all, I don't want to blow his cover by calling him out too soon. If there's something you need me to pass on to him, I'd be glad to.'

Her hands moved to her hips as she studied me. 'If you get my boy in trouble with this undercover business, I'll have your badge. You understand me, Sheriff?'

I wasn't sure what she was gonna *do* with my badge, but I nodded just the same. 'Let me get a message to him,' I said, 'and I'm sure he'll get a chance to get back to you later today.'

'Just tell him to call me. That's all.' With that, Clovis Pettigrew swung around and marched out the door and Gladys and I both breathed a sigh of relief.

Turning to Gladys, I asked, 'Where's Dalton?'

'Hell if I know!' she said, which was one of the very few times I'd ever heard her use a cuss word. But Clovis Pettigrew has that effect on people.

'Find him!' I said.

'Where? He's obviously not at home and he sure as heck isn't here! He doesn't go any place else!' Gladys said.

She had a point. I went back to my office and called up my second-in-command, Emmett Hopkins, who was at home today, since he'd be covering the weekend. I woke him up.

'You know where Dalton is?' I asked him.

'Dalton?' he repeated, sounding sleepy, which made me feel a little bit guilty, but it was a measure of my manhood how quickly I got over it.

'Yeah. We can't seem to find him. You send him out on something?' I asked.

'Uh uh,' Emmett said. 'Haven't talked to Dalton since yesterday morning.' There was a small silence, then he said, 'But he did seem excited about something. When I asked him what, he just said he had a busy weekend coming up.'

'Well, according to his mama he left there yesterday evening, saying he was going undercover and wouldn't be back until Monday,' I told Emmett.

'Say what?' Emmett said. I could hear the bed covers rustling as he got himself up.

'You heard me,' I said.

'Yeah, I heard you, but that's bullshit,' Emmett said.

'*I* know that. I wouldn't use Dalton for anything under-cover. Even if we had anything we needed somebody to go undercover for. I'm thinking he lied to his mama.'

'No shit,' Emmett said. 'Dalton lied to his mama. That's not like him.'

'Tell me about it,' I said.

'So where is he?' Emmett asked.

'Hell if I know.' I hung up without a goodbye and sat at my desk thinking. Dalton had today and the weekend off, told his mama he wouldn't be back until Monday and he wasn't due back here until then. So why was I upset? Dalton was a grown man and if he decided to get away from his mama for a day or two, who could blame him? He'd talked a while back about wanting to get married. He'd said at the time that he didn't have a girlfriend or anything, but that had been a while ago. Didn't mean he didn't have one now. So maybe he was with a woman. That was a good thing. At least to me – doubt his mama would see it that way, though.

I couldn't help thinking back to when Dalton first came on with the sheriff's department. My predecessor, Elberry Blankenship, was sheriff then and him and his wife went to the Church of Christ, where Clovis Pettigrew had dragged her children twice a Sunday – every Sunday of their lives.

At that time, Dalton was twenty-two years old and had held five jobs. Because of his size, when he graduated high school, Bodine's Feed & Grain hired him right up, knowing he was big enough and strong enough to throw around the huge sacks of feed and other stuff Bodine's Feed & Grain sold. That is, until they found out he was very politely not selling deer feeders, deer licks or the very expensive (the prize that kept Bodine's Feed & Grain in the black every year) deer blinds handmade by Lester Bodine, Sr himself. Dalton just didn't believe in shooting animals. He got fired.

Rigsby's Five & Dime fired him because he couldn't

seem to get the price gun to work; and his table-waiting days at the Longbranch Inn concluded after he spilled a cup of coffee, two eggs over easy, grits and biscuits all over His Honor, the Mayor. There was a job at some place over in Bishop that I know didn't last too long, and one in Taylor County that ended in him being asked not to come back that way anytime soon.

It was a grave Clovis Pettigrew who practically begged the sheriff to hire Dalton after the retirement of Dale Morgan, who had dropped dead two days after retirement, which goes to show you either don't retire period or you retire real early so you can enjoy it. Anyway, with great disquiet, the sheriff hired Dalton, mostly for answering the police band radio, which he took to real well. When the sheriff took him out to the shooting range, and gave his own personal gun to him to shoot, he saw that not only was Dalton a crack shot, he didn't shoot a single civilian that popped up on the course. So he sent Dalton up to Oklahoma City for training and got him back six weeks later with a C average in everything but the shooting range, where he made straight A+s. He's been a sworn-in Prophesy County Deputy Sheriff ever since.

I stopped my ruminating and got back to my report, with my last thought on Dalton, 'I hope the boy gets laid.'

CHARLIE SMITH

Charlie Smith liked his new job as police chief of Longbranch, Oklahoma. It beat the hell out of being a homicide detective on the Oklahoma City force. Oklahoma City might not be the biggest city in the country – hell, in the southwest – but it did have its fair share of killings, and although most of them were smoking-gun killings, Charlie didn't believe in misdemeanor murder like a lot of his fellow officers. In fact, Charlie decided to leave the big city force before he got jaded, which was something he saw a lot in his fellow detectives. He wanted to move somewhere where not only was murder a rare thing, but it was also an important thing; a thing that made people sit up and take notice, cry on their neighbor's shoulder and demand justice, no matter who was the victim or the perpetrator.

So he was glad he'd moved to Longbranch, and so were Beth, his wife, and their two girls, Courtney, age nine, and Isabel, age six. The girls loved their new schools and their new teachers – where there had been thirty-three to a class in Oklahoma City, here in Longbranch it was more like 20/1, odds very much in his girls' favor. And Beth, well, Beth just loved it. She'd joined the Methodist Church, something she hadn't been part of since she was a kid, and had just about talked him into at least going. Charlie thought he might talk to the pastor first; he had a few thousand questions on the subject before he let himself get too involved. But best of all, now they were talking about maybe having another kid: that boy Charlie'd been wanting. Well, practice makes perfect, he thought with a grin.

Charlie Smith had what his wife – and other women, truth be known – called a 'shit-eating grin', or, to put it more delicately, a 'cat-ate-the-canary' kind of smile. His teeth were a bit crooked, which somehow added to the charm started by his light brown, almost blond hair, shiny green eyes and tall, lanky, 'I'm a cowboy' body and stride.

He pulled up to the pristine little three-bedroom, two-bath, two-car-garage house in the Meadowbrook Subdivision. White brick with gray-blue trim, the house had a wide, natural wood front door with beveled glass inlay. The little walkway up to the door had two blue pots with an abundance of pansies, and some ivy plants hanging from the little front porch. The yard, he'd noticed, had already been mowed and it wasn't even April yet. The hedges were trimmed, and the grass next to the driveway had a really nice, enviable one-and-a-half-inch straight edge. Somebody knew his fertilizer, Charlie thought.

He normally wouldn't be on a call like this himself, but his boys (and one woman – he wouldn't say girl, no way, no how) were spread pretty thin, and this looked like a pretty cut and dried accident, from the phone-in. He was wearing his uniform shirt over a pair of blue jeans, which he could do since he was the chief. He liked that perk a lot.

The ME's van was already there and the pretty front door was partially open. Charlie rapped on the wood and pushed the door open further, loudly calling out, 'Chief of Police!'

'Back here!' came an answer from a voice he recognized as Dr Rose Church, who his friend Sheriff Milt Kovak referred to as 'the new ME', or Medical Examiner, but who Charlie just thought of as 'the ME' because he'd never met the old one.

Charlie followed the voice back to the master bedroom. A large room, he noted, with a four-poster king-sized bed, big-ass dresser and mirror and a matching chest of drawers. There was even a lounge chair in a corner, just like he used to see in those old 1940s movies his mother liked to watch all the time. Something with Katharine Hepburn and Cary Grant, something like that.

He could see Dr Church's rather large rump sticking out of the bathroom door, but the sobbing he heard coming from the bed stopped him short. The bedclothes were rumpled and a lady sat on the other side of the bed from where Charlie stood. She was facing the bathroom door. She was wearing nightclothes and a bathrobe, and her curly blonde hair was mussed.

'Ma'am?' he said and the lady turned around. It was then that he saw the bathrobe was draped over one arm, which was in a cast and sling. She was a pretty lady, maybe late twenties, early thirties, with what looked to Charlie like natural blonde hair (he didn't see any roots so it had to be, he thought), big, wet blue eyes and one of those mouths that instantly give men dirty thoughts from just looking at.

'Yes, Sir?' she said. He could tell right away that she was a local. There was just a way of talking in this county that pegged him as city-bred the moment he opened his mouth.

'I'm so sorry about your loss.' Charlie went and sat down on the bed next to her, but as far away as the king-sized mattress would let him. 'Is it OK if I ask you some questions?'

The young woman nodded her head and sniffed.

'Your name is Carolina Holcomb?' he asked, and she

nodded her head. 'And the deceased is your husband, Kevin Holcomb?'

Her face crumpled up and a sob broke out of her mouth, but she managed to nod her head.

'Can you tell me what happened here, Miz Holcomb?'

Carolina Holcomb nodded her head once again, took a deep breath and let it out. 'I was in bed 'cause of my arm . . .' she said, indicating the sling. 'I was on pain pills.'

'Can I ask what happened to your arm?' Charlie asked.

'I was in a car wreck yesterday with my girlfriend. We were going shopping.'

Charlie nodded. 'And?'

'You mean today? With Kevin?' she asked, her pretty face scrunching up again as the tears started up.

'Yes, Ma'am. I'm so sorry to be bothering you about this right now, but I gotta.'

She sniffled and nodded her head. Charlie reached across her to a box of Kleenex on the bedside table, handing her one.

She took the offered tissue and thanked him, then sighed. 'Anyway, I was taking a nap. These pain pills . . . You know?'

Charlie nodded in agreement.

'When I woke up, I didn't see Kevin or hear him. He had the day off to look after me. So I called for him 'cause I was thirsty . . .' She gulped in air. 'He didn't answer. And I had to go to the bathroom. The door was closed . . .'

She leaned against Charlie and began sobbing all over again.

Dr Church came out of the bathroom, and Charlie gently moved the girl off his shoulder and got up.

'What'ja got, Doc?' he asked.

She shook her head, then nodded for him to follow her back into the bathroom. As subdivision bathrooms go, it was pretty big, but it was still a stretch for Charlie, Dr Church, Dr Church's assistant and the prone body of Kevin Holcomb.

Dr Church nodded to a bottle of ammonia on top of the toilet and then to a bottle of bleach knocked over on the floor next to the toilet. 'Looks like the poor bastard was trying to clean the bathroom.'

'Well, it's something a man should never do,' Charlie agreed, 'but I never thought of it as a capital offense.'

Dr Church didn't laugh. Charlie knew that it was one of the reasons Milt didn't like her much.

'You mix ammonia and bleach together without proper ventilation and it turns into a lethal gas.' She pointed at the window. 'He didn't even bother to open a window or turn on the vent in here. Not that that would do much good. Most of the vents they put in these houses just move the air around in a circle.'

'No shit?' Charlie said, staring at the vent in the bathroom ceiling. He'd have to check into that when he got home.

'So mixing that stuff killed him, huh?' Charlie asked.

'Dead as a skunk in the middle of the road,' answered Dr Church.

Charlie looked at her, and one corner of her mouth moved a fraction upward. Damn, he thought, I think she made a joke!

'So, you declaring this an accident?' he asked her.

Dr Church shrugged. 'They don't have a spot on the form for stupidity,' she said. 'Gonna have to call it an accident.'

DALTON

Dalton tried lifting his head but it hurt too much. He opened his left eye and peered at his surroundings. There was a Dumpster – a dark blue Dumpster with a bunch of black garbage bags sticking out of it and more on the ground around it. Pavement. The ground was pavement. There were brick buildings. Two of them: one on one side of the pavement and one on the other. One was red brick and the other was kind of orange-colored. He made an executive decision: he was in an alley.

Dalton started to laugh but it hurt his head even more so he stopped. But still, an executive decision: that was pretty funny. He giggled. He tried lifting his head again and it didn't hurt quite as much. He rolled over onto his side, lifting himself up slightly on one elbow. Yes, he was definitely in an alley.

And he wasn't wearing pants.

EMIL

The six months of preparation flew past. There was so much to do, especially when one was motivated, and Dr Emil – excuse me, just Emil Hawthorne (no more medical license, more's the pity) – was extremely motivated. Some of the favors owed to him took a little encouragement to get a return, but he got those returns. Nobody said no to Emil Hawthorne for long.

The man that awoke from the coma was a haggard, withered man. His hair and beard were gray, his muscle tone close to non-existent, his face wrinkled and, most unfortunate of all, his penis flaccid. But there were pills for that. All he needed from those favors owed was money. Lots of money. A hairdresser, a gym, a little Botox here and there and some Viagra, and all that was left was a trip to Barneys Co-op.

When one goes through the process of becoming a psychiatrist, one must go through psychotherapy as part of the training. It was noted by the eminent Dr Stanley Malvern that Emil Hawthorne appeared to lack the ability to accept responsibility for some of his actions. Dr Malvern diagnosed Emil Hawthorne with a personality disorder and recommended that he not be admitted into the psychiatric fellowship he was seeking to join.

Unfortunately, there was a small fire in Dr Malvern's office that month, burning all of his records and catching Dr Malvern there, too. Some said it was arson, although it was never proved. Firefighters rescued the doctor, but regrettably the smoke inhalation caused irrevocable brain damage. Dr Malvern's business partner, Dr Rebecca Hinson, did a rush diagnosis of Emil, and found him quite eligible for his fellowship. The fact that Dr Hinson was under emotional duress due to her secret affair with the now brain-damaged Dr Malvern had more than a little to do with Emil Hawthorne's admittance to the fellowship, which, in turn, led to his internship and thus to his medical degree.

This might have been the reason that Emil Hawthorne blamed only one person for his current situation. Dr Jean MacDonnell.

TWO

MILT

I spent the rest of Friday *not* worrying about Dalton. He was a big boy – an excessively big boy, really – and I figured he could take care of himself, no matter what his mama thought. Mamas tend to underestimate their baby boys' abilities, especially when it comes to women. It's been my experience that mamas of boys tend not to trust their own sex. Of course, daddies of girls are the same way – except *they* usually come armed.

I spent the whole afternoon working on my presentation for the county commissioners on the Mitchem/Highway-5 future traffic light. Then I called my wife. Jean now only worked part-time at the hospital, where she was chief of the psychiatric unit. She was still the chief, but now she had a private practice, in another building, with a partner and a secretary. They'd gotten a loft-like office on the top floor of what used to be Hornscherf's Department Store, located on the square downtown. The bottom floor is now a bookstore/beauty parlor/dress shop, and the top floor houses the psychiatric offices of MacDonnell & Cursey.

The 'Cursey' part of MacDonnell & Cursey was Anne Louise Cursey, MD – a real nice lady Jean had gone to school with back in Chicago. They ran into each other at that psychiatric convention we went to in Las Vegas that time. Since then they kept in touch, and when Anne Louise and her husband got a divorce a while back, she and Jean started talking about her moving to Oklahoma. Anne Louise's son was going off to Rice University in Houston, and it seemed like Longbranch was a heck of a lot closer to Houston than Chicago. And not quite so nasty in the winter.

So they'd set up everything and Anne Louise had moved down here about six months ago, ready to take on the Oklahoma psyche. She was an attractive woman, about Jean's age, with curly, steel gray hair, kinda short and plump, but with a bosom you'd notice a mile away. And I'm not just being a man here, OK? She's got a really gigantic bosom.

I never call Jean's private line unless it's after hours, since she could have someone in her office. Instead, I dialed the main number and got DeSandra Logan, the new secretary. 'O'Donald and Curser,' she said on answering the phone.

'It's MacDonnell and Cursey,' I said.

'Hey, Sheriff,' DeSandra said. 'You wanna speak to Miz O'Donald?'

'Dr MacDonnell,' I corrected.

'She's not in. Well, yes, she is, but she's with a customer,' DeSandra said.

'A patient,' I said.

'Uh huh,' DeSandra said. 'You want me to take a message?'

'Just tell her I called, please,' I answered, as exasperated as I usually feel whenever I speak to DeSandra, the new secretary.

'And who should I say is calling?' DeSandra asked.

I sighed. I could hang up, but then Jean would never know I called. Best to play the game, which, to DeSandra, was no game at all, just horrible reality. 'Her husband,' I said. 'The sheriff.'

'Okey-dokey,' DeSandra said, then hung up on me.

It was a real shame DeSandra was so stupid – excuse me, intellectually challenged. Otherwise, I'd be introducing her to every single man I knew – which wasn't a lot, mostly just Dalton and a couple of guys at the Baptist Church and one or two at Jean's Catholic Church. Because, despite her, ah, intellectually challenged state, she was a real looker. Short black hair in a pixy-like cut, big blue eyes, freckles on her nose, under thirty, tall and thin, with a very nice and very real-looking rack – excuse me, bosom. But all of that faded if you had to listen to her for more than a minute.

With a deep sigh, I got up to go and have my last cup of coffee of the day with the Longbranch police chief, Charlie Smith. We meet at the Longbranch Inn every day, either for lunch or a late afternoon snack. It's usually me, Charlie and my second-in-command, Emmett. Emmett used to have Charlie's job before Emmett had his troubles. But even with that history, Emmett and Charlie get along just fine. Today, though, it was just me and Charlie. It was Emmett's day off, but usually that wouldn't matter – he'd come meet us for some chicken-fried steak and country gravy, whether he was on or not. Or in the afternoon, he'd meet us for one of the Longbranch Inn's famous brownie sundaes that could put a diabetic in a coma in a New York minute. But right now, Emmett's wife Jasmine, another one of my deputies, was on leave – due to the fact that she had just had them a baby girl. These days Emmett had a hard enough time getting out of the house to come to work, much less just to come eat lunch or have an afternoon break with his buds; I'm sure you've heard all about those post-partum things. Hormonal craziness. But please don't tell a lady in that situation that I said so. They tend to be mean.

Charlie and me like to talk about our cases – when we have any – pick each other's brains, so to speak, see if it helps. Since I didn't have anything going except Dalton Pettigrew's mama's lame complaint, it was Charlie's turn.

'Poor woman,' he was saying. 'I felt so sorry for her. Laid up in bed with a lame arm, and her hubby goes and does something nice for her, just helping her out, and it kills him.'

'What'd he do?' I asked.

'Cleaned the bathroom,' Charlie answered.

'Ha!' I said. 'Now if that ain't a reason to leave women's work alone!'

'No shit,' Charlie agreed.

'But I gotta ask, Charlie,' I said. 'How did cleaning the bathroom kill the poor bastard?'

'Got to mixin' his chemicals,' Charlie explained. 'Mixed bleach and ammonia, knocked him right out. Window was shut, vent wasn't on, wife was asleep and he just laid there 'til he died.'

'Man,' I said. 'Rough.'

'How you doin' on your speech for the commissioners?' he asked.

'They're not gonna pay any more attention to this one than they did to the one last year. They just ain't gonna put out the money for that light until there's a dead body.'

'You got a petition?' he asked.

I looked at him.

'A petition, Milt! Hell, when I was in the City, we'd get shit done a lot with the signatures of a couple hundred thousand citizens!'

'We don't have a couple hundred thousand citizens,' I reminded him.

'No, but you got what you got. You get three quarters or even half the voting population of the county to sign a petition, you just watch the commission sit up and take notice.'

A petition, I thought. I could do that.

DALTON

No pants meant no pockets, and no pockets, Dalton thought as he patted his new Jockey undershorts, meant no wallet, no keys, no cell phone, no nothing. He got to his knees; putting his left hand up for support on the wall of the red brick building. It took a moment for the slime his hand landed in to register in his brain. Then he yanked his hand away and almost fell down. He looked around for somewhere to wipe his hand; finding nothing, he opted for his new Jockey undershorts, knowing his mama would throw a wall-eyed fit when she saw whatever it was.

Dalton stood for a moment, looking around the alley.

The sky was dusky looking, but he didn't know if that meant sundown or sunup. Looking at his wrist, he realized his watch was gone; the good watch he'd inherited from his daddy, who'd gotten it from his daddy, who got it upon his retirement from the railroad. Well, Dalton hadn't really *inherited* it from his daddy; his mama just gave it to him one day when he noticed it, saying his daddy must not have been wearing a watch when he abandoned his family.

Dalton sorta wanted to walk to the end of the alley, where he saw the occasional person walk by, maybe ask one of 'em what time it was. But he was afraid the next person to walk by could be a woman with a child, or something like that, and here he was without his pants. I'm certainly in a pickle, Dalton thought.

He put a hand to his head to scratch it, and felt a big bump and crusty dampness. Bringing his hand back down, he saw blood under his fingernails. Thinking things were now getting serious – blood *and* no pants – Dalton decided he needed to try to figure out what was going on. There was a wooden crate by the Dumpster, with a couple of bags of garbage on top of it. Dalton walked over and lifted one of the bags. A large rat ran from between the bags and over his bare feet. He made a screaming noise, not unlike a thirteen-year-old girl seeing her teen rock idol for the first time, and realized simultaneously that not only had a rat just run over his feet, but that his shoes and socks were missing, along with his pants.

Dalton moved the second garbage bag without the help of any rodents, large or small, and sat down, sinking his head into his hands and propping his elbows on his knees. This, he thought to himself, is indeed a pickle.

EMIL

Unfortunately, much as he would have liked to, Emil Hawthorne could not carry out his plan alone. He needed an assistant – a helper, a gofer, an Igor, if you will. He rented a storefront in a soon-to-be-torn-down strip mall in Tulsa, Oklahoma, the closest, well, city, you could say, to

Jean MacDonnell's hideout, and he set out to hire such an entity.

This entity came in the form of one Holly Humphries, the first and only applicant to answer his posting on 'Craig's List'. She was a twenty-five-year-old former video store employee who had been fired for reasons unknown. Holly was tall and thin (although she preferred the term 'svelte'). She smiled a lot, sometimes inappropriately, and Emil considered her stupid enough to do his bidding without question. Especially since she declared that she 'really, really, really' needed the money.

Holly, whose résumé listed her occupation as 'actress' (she'd auditioned for a cable TV show filmed in the area and, although she ultimately didn't get the job, she *had* been called back for a second interview; the closest she'd ever been to an acting job and, therefore, according to Holly, worthy of mention on her résumé), was told by Emil that this *was* an acting gig. Since some of the equipment necessary for Emil's plan included a video camera on a tripod, Holly had not questioned the validity of her new job.

It had taken Emil a while to find the place for his 'location shots'. It had to be near his prey, but far enough away that he wouldn't be found. After his first drive past Jean MacDonnell's house, he had a fairly good lay of the land. Mountain Falls Road was a 5.8-mile stretch from Highway-5 at mile marker seventeen, up Mountain Falls Road, where MacDonnell's house sat nearly at the apex, then down Mountain Falls Road back to Highway-5, just short of mile marker twenty-one. There was an open area near the mile marker twenty-one side, with a dilapidated old building and what looked like trailer hook-ups rusting away. A barely legible sign at the bottom of a path leading back up the mountain into what Emil took to be nothing but a bunch of trees, said, 'TO MOUNTAIN FALLS.'

So, Emil thought, this was actually named *after* something. Although his healing body didn't really feel like it, he took the path leading up the hill. Breathing hard, Emil reached the falls in about twenty minutes of hard hiking. It was nice, he thought, but he'd seen better in his travels.

Before his troubles. He could see all of Highway-5 from here. He could also see two other roads: one leading up the mountain just shy of the mile marker twenty-one side, and one leading up about half a mile from the mile marker seventeen side. It looked like some rough country: plenty of hills, rocky outcrops and all of it covered with trees. But on the mile marker seventeen side, he saw something that looked suspiciously like what he was looking for. A piece of land not as overgrown with trees as the rest, with a barn at the back. No house. Not another house in sight, actually. All the houses he'd seen had been on Mountain Falls Road itself; none on either of the roads cutting through the lower part of the mountain.

He hurriedly took the path back to his rented van and got on Highway-5 at the mile marker twenty-one side, turning left toward Longbranch, in the opposite direction of Tulsa. He took it slow, almost missing the road he'd seen from atop the mountain. It didn't have a name, just a number: County Road 450. It was a gravel road which lead him between heavily forested patches on both sides before he finally found the fence that enclosed the piece of land he'd seen from above. It looked pretty overgrown to him, but he remembered that, from a bird's eye view, you could tell it had once been a farmer's field. Finding the entrance, a mere break between the barbed wire fencing, he saw a faded sign: 'FOR SALE BY OWNER: CALL', and a number so blurred that it was impossible to read.

Emil Hawthorne smiled as he turned his van onto the rutted driveway, heading for the old barn. This is the place, he thought. An old barn, apparently once painted red, but now mostly weathered wood, sat about a quarter of a mile back from the county road. The potholed driveway leading to the barn had high weeds growing up between the two weather-beaten tracks. Weeds grew high all around the barn, including at the entrance to the half-open barn door.

Emil got out of his van and walked up to the barn door. Pushing and pulling, he finally managed to open the other half of the door – that is, if you consider the door falling off its track and landing on the ground as 'open'. He dragged the door so that it was inside the barn, against the wall, and went back to his van for a flashlight. Now armed with a flashlight, he could see that the inside of the barn was a good space. A large, open space with a couple of rotting bales of hay. He just needed a few accessories and it would be perfect.

The next day was Friday, and Emil told his new assistant, Holly, 'We start filming tomorrow.' Holly was a little taken aback. There had been no rehearsal. She worried her improv skills just weren't what they should be. But when he told her they would be leaving for location shots early in the morning, she packed without question.

DALTON

Sarah. It had all been about Sarah. His mind was a little mushy, but he could remember Sarah. How could he not? The love of his life.

On Thursday evening Dalton had driven from Longbranch to Tulsa, excited about seeing Sarah. They were to meet in a coffee shop, a Starbucks, at noon on Friday. He was pretty excited about that. He'd never been to a Starbucks, and it seemed pretty sophisticated to him. Meeting at the Starbucks. Like out of a movie or something. But tonight he was going to stay at a Motel 6. He'd requested a king-sized bed in a no-smoking room on the top floor. It would be his first time alone in a motel room. He'd traveled with his mama and sister and brother to visit his grandparents in Omaha for Christmas, where they'd had to stay at a motel because the house was full once they got there (which pissed off Mama Clovis so much that the next time she'd gone to visit her parents was for the funeral of one, then the other). Once just he and his big brother Hawke had gone to Branson, Missouri for two days as a kind of bachelor party right before Hawke got married, and once he and Anthony Dobbins, another deputy at the sheriff's department, had gone together to Oklahoma City for a conference and stayed three days in a real life hotel, with elevators and restaurants and meeting rooms. It had been the greatest weekend of his life – until this one.

Friday morning he got up and shaved closely, showered, did all those things a man does to impress a lady with his neatness, and was finished and ready to go by nine o'clock.

At eleven, he shaved again, packed his bags, checked out of the motel, got into his car and headed to the Starbucks. He got there early, of course, but it took him a good five minutes to figure out what he wanted to drink. Those drinks were plenty confusing and he had to ask a lot of questions. He knew the people behind him were getting antsy about all his questions, but he wanted to be sure of what he was getting. There were gonna be enough surprises this day, he thought, without having his coffee be a surprise as well.

He finally chose an African blend with a shot of vanilla, heavy steamed cream and put in three sugars himself. He found a table for two, sat down and proceeded to blow on his coffee until it cooled off some. Taking a sip, he decided it was probably the best drink he'd ever put in his mouth. He smiled, thinking this was just the way it was supposed to be – sitting in a Starbucks, waiting for his girlfriend, a fancy coffee drink going smooth down his gullet.

Of course, she wasn't his girlfriend yet, but she was gonna be. He knew that in his heart. This was the real thing, finally. He had almost decided against even looking at his prospective mates after signing up and paying for his 'Mate-Match.' But finally he'd just closed his eyes and hit the button. They'd sent him five profiles with pictures of the ladies. Sarah's picture had stuck out like a rose in a field of dandelions. And her profile was perfect: twenty-five years old, never married, kindergarten teacher, with hobbies that included reading, riding horses, taking long walks and gourmet cooking.

He hadn't been so sure about the gourmet cooking part, but everything else was right up his alley. But now that he'd gotten to know her, if she wanted to fix him some highfalutin meal with lots of forks and such, well, he'd just eat it; that's all there was to it. And he'd smile while he was doing it, too.

And then she'd walked in the door. She was wearing a skirt that fell below her knees, and a sweater set like the one in her picture, but this one was blue, a pale baby blue. The pearls he'd seen in her picture were around her neck, and a pale blue headband held back her blonde hair, more a strawberry-blonde up close and personal. He stood up as she approached, feeling his stomach drop to his toes, afraid that he wouldn't be able to speak at all.

'Dalton?' she said shyly as she reached his table, her throaty voice reminding him of that actress Kathleen Turner, or maybe even his mama's favorite, Lauren Bacall.

'Hey, Sarah,' he managed to get out.

She smiled and he thought he was going to pass out. Her smile was perfect. Her teeth were straight and white, her lips shiny pink. She looked pointedly at the empty chair at his table. 'Oh, please, sit,' he said. She did and he followed suit.

Dalton stuck out his hand to shake hers, thinking that he shoulda done that before they sat down, but better late than never. She took his large hand in her dainty one, the nails polished an almost non-existent pink, the fingers long and slender. Her touch almost made his heart stop. It was like an electric current going through his body. Looking at her face, Dalton figured she must have felt it, too, because they just stared at each other for what must have been half a minute, their hands clasped together. Finally, Sarah broke the physical connection.

Looking down at the table, she said, 'It's very nice to finally meet you face to face.'

'You, too,' Dalton said. Then, seeing his own cup of coffee in front of him, and nothing in front of her, he said, 'Can I get you a cup of coffee?'

Sarah looked up and Dalton got lost again in the blue of her eyes. 'Yes, thank you. I mean, no not coffee, but tea. Chai tea and a packet of *Sweet'N Low*?'

'You got it,' Dalton said, pushing back from the table. Dalton left to fetch her tea, repeating the word 'chai' over and over in his head, lest he forget it and come back with the wrong thing.

It was one of the most wonderful days of Dalton's life. They talked at the Starbucks for an hour, finding out about each other. Somehow Dalton started talking about his father, Threepee; something he never did, not even with family, much less with someone he just met. But it was so easy to talk to Sarah, and in just the time they spent at Starbucks, Dalton felt like he'd known her forever, and known her better than any of his family members.

'And you never saw him again?' Sarah asked, touching his hand after he told her of his father's disappearance.

'Once,' Dalton said. 'Me and my brother Hawke, he's five years older than me, we went to Oklahoma City to buy some supplies we needed to finish up this new bathroom he was building on his house. This was about ten years ago, I guess. And went to the Home Depot up there, and found everything we needed and started to check out. And there he was, right there in front of us. We both recognized him, even from the back. But he never turned around and we never said anything, 'cause, you know, how could we be absolutely sure it was him? And then he left and we saw his profile and it was him, all right. Me and Hawke just looked at each other and Hawke shrugged, but we never said anything about it. Not ever.'

'You and your brother never told anyone about it?' Sarah asked.

'Well, I didn't – not until now. And I don't think Hawke did. 'Course, I wouldn't know, 'cause him and me never discussed it. Ever.'

'Why didn't you tell anyone? And why didn't you speak to your father?' Sarah asked, a pretty frown furrowing her brow.

Dalton shrugged. 'Well, you know, *he* left *us*. Not the other way around. If anybody should be doing any speaking, it should be him speaking to us.'

'But he never saw you,' Sarah said.

Dalton thought about that, recognizing the truth of it. If he'd seen them, would Threepee have spoken? Would he have taken his sons in his arms, dropping his Home Depot purchases to embrace them? Or would he simply have nodded and kept on going? Or maybe not even nodded. Maybe not even recognizing them. It had been a long time: ten years at that time. Twenty now.

Dalton nodded his head. 'That's true,' he said. 'But I just followed Hawke's lead. After my daddy left, Hawke was like my daddy, and I did most things he told me to do. And, well, he didn't speak to him, so neither did I.'

Sarah nodded her head. 'I understand.' She reached for Dalton's hand again and squeezed. 'There's a Chinese restaurant two doors down,' she said. 'Would you like to grab some lunch?'

There wasn't a Chinese restaurant in Longbranch, or in all of Prophesy County, except over in Bishop, where the people with money lived. His mama had fixed Chung King once, but he didn't like it much and she never fixed it again. So if someone were to ask Dalton point-blank, 'Do you like Chinese food?' he would have had to say, 'No.' But Sarah didn't do that. She just said, 'Would you like to grab some lunch?' And he was able to answer truthfully, 'Yes, I would love some lunch.' Not Chinese, but food would be good.

The place was all gussied up Oriental-like, with one wall covered in a picture of the Great Wall of China. There were paper lanterns hanging from the ceiling, and Buddhas everywhere. Right in the middle of the room was a gigantic aquarium that went from floor to ceiling, filled with the most wondrous and beautiful fish he'd ever seen – bright blue fish, yellow fish, little fish with huge, fluffy-looking tails.

'That's a saltwater aquarium,' Sarah said as they sat down. 'Saltwater fish are a lot more colorful than freshwater, aren't they?'

'Yes, Ma'am,' Dalton said, mesmerized by the aquarium.

'Do you know what you want, or would you like me to order for you? I've been here before,' Sarah said.

Relief flooded through Dalton. 'Yeah, you order. That would be great. Thanks.'

The food started coming right away. First, soup with stuff in it he didn't even *want* to identify, but it was spicy like good Mexican food and he couldn't say he didn't enjoy it. Then little pieces of toast with cut-up shrimp and little puffy things that you broke open and inside was cream cheese and crab. He was beginning to think he might like Chinese food.

Then came the entrée. Dalton just stared. Some things he recognized: like the shrimp and the tiny baby ears of corn, which he thought were pretty cool, and the great big red peppers that he was a little curious about. But there were other things he'd never seen before. He decided to hell with his lack of knowledge, and asked Sarah, 'What's this?'

'A scallop,' she said. 'It's a shellfish.'

'And this?' he asked, using his fork to point at something with legs.

Sarah grinned. 'A squid?'

Dalton pulled his fork away from it. 'Like an octopus?'

'Well, no, an octopus is an octopus and a squid is a squid,' she said.

'Yeah, but they both live in the ocean and got too many legs, right?'

Sarah laughed. 'Well, you got me there! Yes, it's just like an octopus.'

'And you're suppose to eat it?' Dalton asked.

'Millions of people do,' she said, taking one off the large serving tray and popping it in her mouth.

'What does it taste like?' Dalton asked, leaning forward as she chewed.

'Seriously?' Sarah asked.

'Yeah,' Dalton said. 'Seriously.'

Leaning in as well, Sarah whispered, 'An art gum eraser, but don't tell anybody I said that, OK?'

Dalton grinned and speared himself a shrimp.

MILT

I got up to my house on Mountain Falls Road that Friday evening around six o'clock, before Jean and Johnny Mac got home. Johnny Mac went to preschool until noon every day, then Jean picked him up and they went to lunch, sometimes fast food, sometimes a picnic in the park – and in the afternoon he went to the hospital with her, staying in the little day care they have for employees' kids. He had friends at both places and seemed to be thriving with his new schedule.

I walked in the house and into the kitchen, where Jean had left out some meat to defrost. I loved the nights I got home before Jean because we had a rule that whoever got home first cooked, and whoever cooked got to cook whatever they wanted. I looked at the skinless, boneless chicken breasts Jean had left out and could only think of one thing: rabbit-fried chicken. This was one of my mama's specialties that I dearly loved, and I hadn't had it in twenty years.

What you do is you dredge the chicken in milk and flour, then fry it like you would normal fried chicken, then put it aside. In the leavings, you mix milk and cornstarch to make cream gravy and add lots of pepper, of course. Then you take the fried chicken and plop it back in the pan, making sure it gets the cream gravy all over it, let it cook a little longer so the gravy soaks in good, then you serve it along with mashed potatoes and a can of green beans. Real good eating.

While I was making the chicken, my mind got to wondering about what Charlie Smith had told me earlier in the day. Seemed strange. Seemed familiar *and* strange. Then I remembered. Had to be fifteen, twenty years back, we had a case just like that. Man at home alone, cleaning the bathroom. I mean if that doesn't prove cleaning toilets is a woman's job, I don't know what does.

Just then Johnny Mac came running in the front door, yelling, 'Daddy! Daddy!'

Ya gotta love it. I picked him up on the fly, swung him around, yelling, 'Johnny Mac!' right back as loud as I could. He belly-laughed at that one, like he always did. It was a thing we did. A father–son thing. A guy thing.

'What are you cooking?' Jean asked, suspicion in her voice. Jean has this thing about fried foods: she thinks they'll kill you. Flat out kill you. She lifted the lid on the frying pan and looked in at the wonder that is rabbit-fried chicken. Glancing back at me, she raised one eyebrow. That was a killer thing she did, raising that one eyebrow. Depending on what was going on, it could mean several things: 'You randy?' (meaning me, of course), 'You said what?' (again, me) or, in this case, 'What the hell is this?'

'Rabbit-fried chicken,' I answered her unspoken question. 'Fried is just an expression in this case,' I tried to assure her.

Again, the eyebrow.

This new eyebrow meant she wasn't buying it.

'I swear you're gonna love it,' I said, going back to the stove. 'And we hardly ever have anything fried. Just this once isn't going to kill us.'

Without answering (I mean, how could she argue with that kind of logic, right?), she walked right through the kitchen and into our bedroom.

I was serving up plates when the phone rang. We've got an extension in the kitchen and I picked it up after the first ring. 'Sheriff Kovak,' I said.

'Sheriff, I still haven't heard from Dalton,' came Clovis Pettigrew's unpleasant nasal twang.

'Well, Ma'am,' I said, stretching out the long cord as I placed Johnny Mac's plastic divider plate at his place at the table. 'I tried to get the message to him, but when somebody's undercover, it's kinda hard to know whether or not they got the message . . .'

'Now you listen to me, Sheriff,' she said. 'You got no call putting Dalton in harm's way like that! Dalton's a deputy, not some *dee*-tective you put undercover with prostitute trash and drug dealers and such. He better not be consorting with prostitutes and drug dealers!'

'No, Ma'am,' I said, thinking on the fly. 'It's not that sort of case.'

'Then what sort of case is it?' she demanded.

'I'm not at liberty to say,' I said, liking the sound of that. I thought about saying, 'It's on a need to know basis,' or 'If I told you, I'd have to kill you,' but thought that might be a little over the top.

'I'm giving you ten minutes, Sheriff, to produce my son,' Miz Pettigrew said, 'then I'm going to . . .'

She stopped. Even Clovis Pettigrew didn't know what to do at this point. Call the Feds? Sic her preacher on me? Tell my mama?

'Ma'am,' I said, letting her off the hook. 'I'm not sure
if Dalton will be able to call tonight, but I'm sure we'll
hear from him in the morning and I'll have him call you
first thing.'

'You do that!' Clovis Pettigrew said and slammed the
phone down in my ear.

All I could think at that point was that Dalton was going
to get a piece of my mind come Monday morning – or
whenever he called.

THREE

DALTON

After eating lunch together and talking all this personal
talk, Dalton hoped Sarah felt safe enough to say yes
when he said, 'I don't know Tulsa that well. If you'd
like, I'd love to take a tour in my truck with you as my
guide.'

Sarah smiled. 'I'd love it.'

They went to the Will Rogers Museum and Birthplace,
and the Oklahoma Jazz Hall of Fame. Dalton, of course,
knew who Will Rogers was – everybody in Oklahoma knew
that – but he had no idea there was a Jazz Hall of Fame,
or so many jazz musicians from Oklahoma.

As they drove around the city, Dalton had to stop his truck
at the sight of a humongous pair of bronze praying hands.

'My goodness,' he said to his tour guide. 'What's that?'

'Oral Roberts University,' Sarah answered. 'You
remember? The man who said he saw a nine-hundred-foot
Jesus who told him to build his hospital?'

'Oh, yeah. I know him. I mean, I know who he is. Mama
said he used to heal people.'

'That's what I hear,' Sarah said, laughing slightly.

'You don't believe in healing?' Dalton asked.

'Well,' Sarah was obviously thinking about it. 'I do believe
God can heal, but I don't think he does it by having some

man make money by putting his hands on people and shoving them.'

Dalton thought about that for a moment, then started up his truck again and pulled back onto the road. 'You're probably right.'

JEAN MACDONNELL

Saturday morning dawned beautiful and bright; a spring day right out of a picture book, more a Midwest spring than an Oklahoma spring, Jean thought. Knowing where she was, though, she knew that the spring would be shorter here than back home, and the heat would be all-consuming in less than two months. She doubted that she'd ever get used to an Oklahoma summer.

She and John had a noon birthday party to go to, held at City Park, which was certainly the right place for a day like this. The party was to celebrate the fifth birthday of one of John's classmates at day care, another pre-K student: a little girl named Arletta. Mother and son had already spent way too much time at Wal-Mart 'discussing' whether Arletta would prefer the new Princess Barbie or a really cool Optimus Prime Transformer. Jean won with the Princess Barbie.

John was four now and insisted on picking out his own clothes. Jean knew she had to let him, realizing that her reluctance was merely her desire to keep him a baby as long as possible. Sometimes, she thought, knowing this crap is a pain in the ass.

John picked out his Transformer T-shirt, a pair of denim shorts, socks and his light-up, glow-in-the-dark Batman running shoes.

'You're a vision,' Jean told him.

'Huh?' he asked, slipping on his second shoe.

She laughed and rubbed his head. 'Nothing, big guy. Go say 'bye to Daddy.'

Last shoe on, he ran through his bedroom door like his pants were on fire, running down the stairs, yelling, 'Daddy!' at the top of his lungs. Jean cringed as she watched her young son bolt down the steep staircase, knowing she had to let him. 'Keep him safe from the big boo-boos,' she told herself almost constantly. 'The little boo-boos make him stronger.'

As John headed down the stairs in search of his father, Jean called out, 'Don't forget Arletta's present, John!'

He stopped dramatically in his tracks and whirled around. He went running into the dining room, where the Disney princess bag, with glittery pink tissue paper sticking out, sat, awaiting its trip to the party. John grabbed it, swung it over his head, yelled, 'Come on, Mom!' and headed out the door.

Sighing while she laughed, Jean followed. Even though the weather was perfect at that moment, Jean grabbed sweaters for both her and John, since late March in this part of Oklahoma meant the weather could change at any given moment.

Milt was outside, peering at the engine of his Jeep.

'What's wrong?' Jean asked.

'Nothing,' he said. 'Kinda sluggish.'

'Take it to a mechanic,' Jean suggested.

'I did all the work on my fifty-five myself,' Milt said, not looking at his wife.

'This isn't the fifty-five. This has a catalytic converter. A computer. This is an actual modern car.'

'You really think this calls for sarcasm?' inquired Milt.

Jean raised an eyebrow as she lifted John into the back seat of her Volvo.

Milt walked over to Jean's car and helped buckle John into his car seat. 'You gonna be good at the party?' Milt asked.

'Yes, Sir,' John answered.

'You gonna listen to your mama?' Milt asked.

'Yes, Sir,' John answered.

'You gonna fly home on a unicorn?' Milt asked.

John laughed and rolled his eyes. 'Daddy!'

Milt kissed his son, then his wife, and closed her door. 'Be careful,' he said, touching her hand where it rested in the open window.

'Always,' she said, smiling at him. She finger-waved a goodbye and they were off.

It was a good five miles to City Park, once they were off the mountain. In Longbranch, five miles was a big deal. Jean pulled the Volvo up as close as she could to the picnic table that was spread with goodies and a sign reading, HAPPY BIRTHDAY, ARLETTA. Grabbing her purse, her crutches, her son and the Barbie, Jean headed into the fray.

HOLLY HUMPHRIES

He'd dumped her in a barn so far out in the country that Holly had no idea where she was. It was pretty – but everything looked exactly the same and had for the last half hour. Green trees, big hills and wild flowers, mile after mile after mile. All fairly foreign stuff to this Tulsa-bred city girl.

Once inside the barn, she saw camera equipment, some props, a cot, a couple of director's chairs and a table with an ice chest and water jug.

Holly had wanted to ask, 'Hey, where you going?' when Mr Smith dropped her off, but Holly didn't think his demeanor lent itself to questions. She sat down in one of the director's chairs, head in hand, elbow on knee, and thought that what she'd always heard about acting was true: just a lot of sitting around and waiting.

EMIL

Leaving his new assistant alone in the barn, Emil Hawthorne drove the rented van out to Highway-5 and up what he already thought of as the backside of the mountain — the end of the road closest to Tulsa. He drove up Mountain Falls Road and slowly past Jean MacDonnell's house. The Jeep was in the driveway, but her minivan was not. Emil smiled. This was the time. Things were going to work out perfectly.

He had already found a clearing about twenty yards from Jean MacDonnell's driveway, on the opposite side, if she was to be coming from Longbranch, which he figured she would be. The clearing was surrounded with trees and, having already checked during the day when both Jean and her husband were at work, he knew his van could not be seen by someone turning into their driveway, unless they craned their necks. However, from his location in the clearing, he could see her driveway perfectly.

He kept going in the direction that he was headed, down Mountain Falls Road toward Highway-5, where he turned right onto Highway-5, on to the other entrance to Mountain Falls Road and back up the mountain to his hidey-hole. He sat there in the van, shaking with anticipation. It wouldn't be long now, he thought. Not long at all.

DALTON

Sarah directed Dalton to Riverbanks Park, on the banks of the Arkansas River that ran near the downtown area, and they parked his truck and walked along the newly renovated river's edge, passing the floating stage and amphitheater in the middle of the river. Although the sun was shining and the sky was blue, it was still only mid-March and there was a chilly wind blowing off the river toward them, blowing an odor of rotting fish and decay. Neither mentioned it, concentrating instead on the flowers in neat borders along the walkway, brilliant colors reaching for the sky.

'I guess I never knew Tulsa was so pretty,' Dalton said, looking down at Sarah and wishing he had the nerve to hold her hand. That would be really nice, he thought, walking along the river's edge, holding hands with this pretty girl.

'The city's been doing a lot of renovations over the years,' Sarah said. 'I think they're actually getting it right.'

Making it back to the truck, they drove to Cherry Street and then walked along admiring the small shops and checking out the menus at the many restaurants.

'Oh, look at this shop!' Sarah said, pointing in the window of a shop that seemed to specialize in eclectic items from all over the world. 'May we go in here?' Sarah asked.

Dalton felt himself preening inside. He'd never been around anyone, man or woman, who said 'may' instead of 'can'. He knew the difference and knew Sarah had done it right! She is so refined, he thought. And what a great teacher she must be for little kids. He couldn't wait for her to start teaching their children the difference between 'may' and 'can'.

They walked into the store, the smell of patchouli incense almost knocking Dalton over. The store was so crowded, Dalton worried about knocking stuff over because of his size. He tried slipping sideways through the aisles so he wouldn't hit anything. There was stuff from the Middle East, stuff from the Orient and stuff from right there in Tulsa: home-made stuff. Candles and paintings and vases and sculpture and jewelry.

Sarah found a scarf, a big one, made of some silky kind of material and studded with sequins and beads and other doodads Dalton didn't recognize. It was black at one end and faded to an aqua blue at the other.

'Oh, I have to have this!' Sarah said.

'I'll get it for you,' Dalton said, wondering how much something like that would cost.

'Oh, no! Never. I've got it.'

Realizing it was already six thirty, they found a restaurant with a tantalizing menu (at least to Sarah) and went inside for dinner. Dalton knew how to read, but he just didn't understand anything the menu said. Not wanting to look totally stupid, he said, 'This is your city. Why don't you order for both of us?' He heard that line in a movie once. It was the girl saying it, but still . . .

'You sure?' Sarah asked, smiling at him.

'Absolutely,' Dalton answered, smiling back.

And so she did. The appetizer they shared was called a 'cauliflower latke' when she'd ordered it, but it turned out in real life to be a potato pancake with spicy green sauce. He'd told her he liked beef so she'd ordered him a steak and mac and cheese. Except the mac and cheese had lobster in it and the carrots were spicy hot and sitting next to some green stuff that tasted like licorice, something he'd never liked. His first instinct was to spit it out, but he'd stopped doing that in high school.

'You don't like the braised fennel?' Sarah asked.

'What's that?'

She pointed at the green stuff. Dalton shook his head apologetically, 'Sorry. It takes like licorice,'he said.

'You want to try some of mine?' she asked.

Dalton looked at her bacon-wrapped duck breast, sitting on what looked like baby food, and declined the invitation. As far as Dalton was concerned, the best part of the meal was the apple martinis Sarah kept ordering. They were, in his opinion, damn good.

When the bill came, Dalton thought he might pass out from sticker shock, but managed to put down his Visa card like he knew what he was doing. He figured it would take two months to pay off this dinner.

As they walked back to his truck, Dalton asked shyly, 'Do you need to go home or be somewhere?'

Sarah smiled. 'No,' she said. 'Nowhere without you.'

Dalton smiled back.

Sarah directed him to a club she said she'd heard about. There they switched to mojitos. It was around midnight when Sarah took Dalton's hand in hers and said, 'I never thought I'd find a man so understanding. So macho. So gorgeous.'

Dalton blushed. 'Well, you're really pretty.'

'Thank you,' Sarah said, smiling widely at him. Her shyness had diminished with the cocktails, Dalton noted. But then, so had his. Dalton reached forward and cupped the back of Sarah's head, bringing her face toward him, and kissed her. Closed mouth, since it was the first kiss, and tender, but not a peck. *Definitely* not a peck.

When he released her, Sarah sat back in her chair and fanned her face with her hand. 'Whew!' she said. 'Mama, buy me that!'

Dalton laughed.

'You know,' Sarah said, leaning forward and taking Dalton's hand in hers, 'you just don't seem the type to be into trannies.'

'Well,' Dalton said, 'I prefer working on an engine block, and even brakes, but trannies are OK.'

'What?' Sarah said.

Dalton had almost forgotten Sarah's earlier mention in her emails that she was a 'trannie'. A new word, Dalton figured, for people who liked to work on automobile transmissions. She seemed like such a girly girl, but you never could tell these days.

'Transmissions are OK. Little detailed, you know, but maybe not as detailed as working on a brake system, or a catalytic converter, or something like that,' Dalton said, smiling at this beautiful girl in front of him.

Sarah took her hand out of Dalton's and fell back into her chair. *'Transmissions?'* she said.

'Yeah?' Dalton wondered why she seemed so sad all of a sudden.

'Excuse me,' Sarah said, and left.

Dalton watched her leave, taking her oversized purse with her, and his imagination went into overdrive – just like a well-built transmission. Her hips were a little on the small side, but he thought how small his mama was, and she had three real big babies. He figured Sarah could pop 'em out with no problem. And right away. He wanted babies right away. As she disappeared down the hall toward the restrooms, Dalton turned back to his table and finished his third mojito, holding up the empty glass to the waitress to signal for another. He wouldn't mention anything about babies right away, of course, not even about marriage. But maybe by the end of the weekend. That would be the time, he thought.

'Put it on my tab,' he told the waitress — the same way that Sarah had for their last round. He giggled as the waitress walked off. 'Put it on my tab!' he repeated, giggling some more.

Then someone came and sat down at his table. Someone he didn't know. 'That seat's saved,' Dalton told him.

'I know,' the man said.

Dalton frowned as he looked down at his mojito and then inhaled half of it. There's something familiar about this guy, he thought. But Dalton was sure he didn't know him from Adam.

'Dalton,' the man said.

'Seat's saved . . . How'd you know my name?'

'Dalton, you need to concentrate here,' the man said.

'My girlfriend's gonna be back any minute,' Dalton said. 'Well, she's not exactly my girlfriend – not yet anyway – but she's gonna . . . Who are you?' he asked, signaling to a waiter for another round.

The man pulled Dalton's hand down. 'I think you've had enough.'

'Whoa now!' Dalton said, jerking his hand out of the man's grip. 'Don't you go grabbing! I want another drink!'

'I think you've had enough to drink,' the man said.

'Who are you, the drink police? Where's Sarah?' Dalton asked, trying to stand from his chair but not making it all the way up.

'I'm right here, Dalton,' the man said, swinging Sarah's extra-large purse up onto the table.

Dalton looked all around but couldn't find the girl of his dreams. 'Where is she?' he whined, staring at Sarah's purse. 'What did you do with her?'

The man touched Dalton's hand where it rested on the table. 'I'm right here,' he said again, pulling a strawberry-blonde wig out of the oversized purse.

Dalton jerked his hand away. 'Huh?'

'I thought you understood!' the man said, tears in his eyes. 'I thought you knew what "trannie" meant!'

'Wha—?' Dalton said, shaking his head. 'Transmission? Yeah, I know what it means! Makes the car go!'

The man took a deep breath and then let it out. Finally, he said, 'No, Dalton, it means men who like to dress up like women.'

'Huh?' Dalton said again.

The man sighed and held out his hand, 'Hi, I'm Geoffrey.'

MILT

It was kinda nice having the house to myself on a Saturday, even if only for a couple of hours. More than that and it would probably get lonely. It's funny how fast you can get used to the carryings-on of a four-year-old. I can't believe I went almost sixty years before becoming a daddy. Something I shoulda done at least thirty years ago. Except then the mama woulda been my ex-wife LaDonna, which is a whole 'nother ball of wax.

I called Virgil Wynn down at the Exxon station, set up an appointment to get the Jeep looked at on Monday and to get a ride to the sheriff's office, then wandered back outside to my new garage.

There was a time when this cleared section of my property had a small stable and a fenced-in area for horses, except that when I bought the place, I didn't have any horses. Then a tornado knocked that down, and my sister and her kids were still living here and I thought maybe I'd build a pool. But before I got that notion totally clear in my head, my sister up and married and moved her and her kids to Bishop, on the other side of the county. So then when me and Jean got married, and we knew we were having a baby, she — I mean *we* — decided a pool wouldn't be a good idea. That's when I had the garage built. Not only is it a garage, it's a workshop, too. Fits two cars and a boat, if I ever get one, and has a room all along the back set up for woodworking and general manly messing around. *And* it has an air conditioner. So I wandered out there and put my tools in alphabetical order.

My cell phone rang when I was on the 'D's – drill, drill bits, Dustbuster, drummet. I picked it up and said, 'Hello'.

'Did you find him?' Clovis Pettigrew demanded.

I sighed. 'Not yet, Ma'am. But he'll call in soon, I swear.'

She hung up loudly in my ear. Which I felt was better than having to listen to her.

DALTON

'Honey, what'ja doing out here without your pants on?' a voice said.

Dalton jerked his head up. There was a woman at the end of the alleyway. Well, at least he *thought* it was a woman. She had on a real short skirt with high red boots, a real low top showing what looked like real boobies and big blonde hair. The hair he figured wasn't real 'cause her skin was the color of black coffee.

'You a real woman?' Dalton asked.

'Real as heartbreak, honey.' She moved toward him and Dalton could see that those boobies sure *looked* real. Still being a little on the drunk side, he reached out and touched one as she bent over him. She cupped his hand so that it squeezed her breast. 'Now you feel that, baby? Them phony ones don't feel soft like that now, do they, baby?'

Dalton pulled his hand away and blushed. 'Sorry, Ma'am,' he said, trying to get up.

'Here, baby, let me help you,' the woman said, pulling him to his feet. 'How'd you get out here in your underpants?'

Dalton shook his head. ''Don't know. I was in a club, talking to somebody, last I remember.'

'Baby, you got any money?' she asked, cradling his left arm between her breasts.

Dalton looked down at his undershorts. 'Don't reckon I do,' he said.

The woman sighed. 'That's a real shame. I like me a big ol' white boy ever once in a while, know what I mean?'

'Ma'am?' Dalton asked.

The woman laughed. 'Come on, honey,' she said, pulling at his arm. 'Let's go get you some coffee.' She headed for the street at the end of the alley.

Dalton pulled back. 'Oh, no, Ma'am! I can't go out there. I don't have my pants on!'

'Hey, Tanjene!' called a male voice from the other end of the alley.

The woman looked behind Dalton and made a face. 'Yo, Luther. What'ja doing back here? Told you no more freebies!'

'Ah, Tanjene, honey . . .'

'Hey, Luther, listen up. Gimme your pants and I'll think about a BJ later tonight. How's that sound?'

'OK,' the man said, taking off his pants and handing them over without question.

Tanjene held them out to Dalton. 'Put these on, honey,' she said.

Dalton looked at the pants. They were a black, white and orange plaid. The shirt he was wearing was a Western-cut dark blue paisley and white. ''Don't know if these are gonna fit,' he said, looking at Tanjene.

'So they might be a little short, honey. Good enough to get you some coffee, don'ja think?'

Dalton pulled on the pants. He couldn't fasten them at the waist, as they were too small, so Tanjene pulled his paisley shirt down over the open fly. The cuffs stopped three inches above his ankles. His feet were still bare. Tanjene looked at Dalton's feet and then at Luther's, and shook her head. 'Baby, you gonna have to go barefoot, all there is to it.'

'Yes, Ma'am,' Dalton said, glancing at Luther's feet himself. Dalton wore a size-thirteen shoe; not many people even got close to that.

'Luther, you go on home and get you some more pants. Can't be walking around half-naked like that!' Tanjene said over her shoulder as she walked Dalton out of the alley.

'But you said—' Luther started.

Tanjene cut him off. 'I said later, Luther, now didn't I? Is this later? I don't *think* so!' She turned back around and hugged Dalton's arm to her breasts. 'Come on, honey, let's get out of this stinky old alley!'

EMIL

He had a plan. It was fairly simple and straightforward. No one would get hurt, but Dr Jean MacDonnell would suffer, of that he was certain. He just wasn't sure how long he could make her suffer. Days? Weeks? Surely not months. There was only so much a man could take.

Sitting in his van, tucked under some trees only yards from Jean's driveway, he watched. It was quiet up here on the mountain; very nice. *Too* nice. She had a good life here, he thought. But he would soon change that.

JEAN MACDONNELL

Jean sat at the picnic table beside the only other woman she knew at the party, Mary Ellen Knight, the sister of Milt's deputy Dalton Pettigrew. Mary Ellen's son Eli was in the same group at day care as John. Jean attempted to carry on a polite conversation with Mary Ellen, but it was difficult because the other woman would start a sentence and then let it peter out into nothingness, never actually finishing a thought. Jean thought that the woman was obviously suffering from severe clinical depression. However, Jean tried to never make a diagnosis in a social setting, although, like now, it was often hard not to.

'So where do you work?' Jean asked after they'd discussed their children ad nauseam.

'At Sinclair's?' Mary Ellen said, making it sound as if she was asking Jean for the truth of the fact.

Jean shook her head. 'I'm not sure what that is.'

'Oilfield supply?' Mary Ellen offered.

'Oh,' Jean said, trying a smile. 'What do you do there?'

Mary Ellen was quiet for a moment, as if considering, then she said, 'I'm a credit representative.'

'Oh,' Jean responded, 'that must be interesting.'

'Not really,' Mary Ellen said.

Silence ensued.

'I'm a psychiatrist,' Jean said finally, feeling like an idiot when the words came out of her mouth.

'Yes,' Mary Ellen nodded.

Finally, the birthday girl's father got the piñata hanging correctly up in the tree and the children began their blindfolded attempts at whacking it. Jean felt this was the perfect opportunity to forego the conversation with Mary Ellen. She stood up on her crutches and began rooting for the next child in line.

DALTON

Tanjene had barely managed to walk Dalton through the mouth of the alley when she was jerked sideways by a man in baggy jeans, an oversized T-shirt and so much gold around his neck that it made Dalton dizzy. He looked like one of those rappers you see on TV, except that he was a white man.

'Where you been, ho?' the white man shouted at Tanjene, almost picking her up off her feet with his grip on her upper arm.

'Nowhere, J.M. I swear . . .'

'Who this honky? I tell you to take this honky? I don't think so!' the white man yelled.

'J.M., I talked to that man you wanted me to, but he wasn't interested, I swear . . .'

The man called J.M. slapped Tanjene hard across the face. And Dalton laid him out on the sidewalk.

'Wha' the fuck . . .' J.M. said from his position lying on his back on the hard concrete of the sidewalk.

'You don't hit a lady!' Dalton said, standing over J.M., fists still clinched, more from the pain in his head than from any residual anger.

'Well, I ever see a lady round here, I won't do that!' J.M. said. 'Now, sucker, you gonna die!'

J.M. jumped to his feet, a switchblade in his hand.

JEAN

Jean had moved as far away from Mary Ellen Knight as she could, getting closer to the piñata so that she could watch John as he whacked at it blindfolded. She felt blindfolds were a little much for four-year-olds, but then she thought it possible she was coddling her son again. She sighed. 'Little boo-boos, little boo-boos,' she said to herself, her new mother's mantra.

John had just finished his third swing, actually touching the piñata this time, when Mary Ellen touched Jean's arm. Jean was busy clapping, leaning her underarms on the cushioned tops of her crutches.

Jean turned her head at the intrusion. 'Hey, Mary Ellen,' she said and smiled.

Mary Ellen didn't smile back. 'I've got a family emergency,' she said, her voice flat. 'Will you take Eli home with you and I'll have my husband pick him up later?'

'Of course,' Jean said. 'Is there anything I can do to help?'

'No,' Mary Ellen said, and turned to her son, directly behind her. 'Eli, stay with John's mama. Daddy'll come get you at John's house, OK?'

'OK, Mama,' Eli said, then ran toward the throng of children, yelling, 'Hey, John, guess what?'

Mary Ellen nodded her head, then walked toward her minivan.

The party was over less than an hour later, and Jean bundled both boys into the car. John was still in a car seat, the 'big boy's car seat', they called it, but they only had one. So Jean took it out, putting it in the trunk of the Volvo, and put both boys in shoulder harnesses.

It was close to three o'clock by the time she pulled into the driveway. Milt came out of the garage to meet them. Getting out of the driver's side, Jean said, 'We've got company.'

Eli jumped out of his side of the car and shouted, 'Howdy, Sheriff!'

'Well, howdy yourself, Eli! What're you doing here?'

Eli shrugged. 'Mama said come, so I came.'

Milt shrugged back. 'What's a man to do, huh?'

'Yes, Sir,' Eli said, willing to agree with anything the sheriff said.

'Your turn,' Jean said. 'I'm going in to take a long, hot bath.'

'That bad, huh?' Milt asked.

Jean just rolled her eyes and went into the house.

'Well, you guys come on in the garage and we'll build something. What do you say?'

'Yeah!' Johnny Mac shouted. 'Come on, Eli!'

'Yeah!' Eli shouted back and they ran inside.

Once inside, though, Eli said, 'I forgot my breathie in the car!'

'What's a breathie?' Milt asked.

Eli made a motion as if using an inhaler, and Milt said, 'You got asthma?'

'Yes, Sir. My breathie's in the car!'

'Let me go get—'

'I'll get it!' Eli shouted. 'I can open the door all by myself!'

He ran out of the garage and Milt chuckled to himself. They grow up so quick. He bent down to show his son how to put something in the vice.

FOUR

EMIL

It was lush up here on top of the mountain. Pretty. Lots of oaks and pines up here, and in the quiet, during the lulls between bird calls, he could hear the far-off babbling of the falls, where Mountain Falls Road got its name. The two-lane blacktop was quiet, hardly another car traveling along it in the time Emil sat there. Then he heard one coming. He slid down in his seat, his eyes barely peaking over the window opening.

It was a Volvo – just like the one registered to Jean MacDonnell. After watching the car pull into her driveway, Emil got out of the van and made his way through the trees and brush to the clearing in front of the house. A two-story, white stucco house. The first stucco house he'd actually seen in Oklahoma. A white metal three-car garage to the right of the house, its bay doors open.

While he was checking it out, the boy ran out of the garage, heading for the car. Emil couldn't believe his luck. He thought the stars were certainly shining on his enterprise. Handing the boy to him like a gift.

DALTON

The thrust of the switchblade barely missed Dalton as he rolled quickly to his left. J.M. fell and Dalton jumped him, pinning his knife hand to the sidewalk.

'Drop it!' Dalton shouted. 'I'm a sheriff's deputy and you don't wanna be messin' with me!'

'Ah, fuck, Tanjene!' J.M. said, dropping the knife and turning his head toward the woman.

'I din' know, J.M., I swear.' Turning to Dalton, she said, 'Look, mister, he din' mean nothin'. He was just messin' with you.' She tried a smile. 'Right, J.M.?'

J.M. turned a painful grin toward Dalton. 'Yeah, man, just messin' wid you. I wasn' gonna hurt you none, swear, man.'

'You have the right to remain silent . . .' Dalton was saying.

'Oh, man, don't go arrestin' him!' Tanjene whined. 'It'll take ever dime I got to get him out! Then he's gonna beat my ass 'cause I don't got any money today!'

'Tanjene!' J.M. wailed. 'You ain't helping!'

Tanjene tugged on Dalton's arm. 'Please, mister, let him go. For me? I got you them pants and everthing!'

Dalton looked at the woman in the blonde wig. One, he had no jurisdiction here and he'd end up having to drag this guy all over hell and gone since he didn't know where the police station was; and two, he didn't know where his car was, which meant walking this guy up and down looking for it, with Tanjene whining the whole way; and three, his head hurt and he didn't have any handcuffs.

Dalton pocketed the switchblade and stood up, taking his weight off J.M.

'Get up,' Dalton said to him.

J.M. got carefully to his feet, Tanjene helping by pulling at his arm. He shook her off.

'You ain't gonna take me in?' J.M. asked suspiciously.

'No,' Dalton said.

'You think I gonna give you a freebie with Tanjene here 'cause of that?'

Dalton's eyes widened and he looked from one to the other. 'You ain't her boyfriend?' Dalton asked.

Tanjene rolled her eyes. 'I saw that!' J.M. accused.

'He my pimp,' Tanjene said, turning toward Dalton.

'Hush up, girl!' J.M. said, pulling his arm back in a threatening manner.

Dalton cupped his bear claw of a hand over J.M.'s upraised fist. 'We're not going through this again,' he said. 'I'll call the police, have 'em come get your ass.'

J.M. laughed and looked Dalton up and down. 'In them pants? They arrest you, not me!'

Dalton pushed the man away. 'Get going. Now!'

Still laughing, J.M. sauntered off, backing down but keeping his pride intact.

MILT

It seemed to be taking Eli way too long to get his 'breathie'. I told Johnny Mac, 'Stay here a minute,' and walked to the Volvo sitting in the driveway. It was empty. Thinking that he'd gone into the house for a drink or something, I went back and got Johnny Mac and took him with me into the house, thinking I never should have let Eli go after his 'breathie' alone. Shit, the boy was only four, same as Johnny Mac. What the hell was I thinking?

Johnny Mac and I walked in the front door, and I hollered, 'Eli! Hey, boy, where are you?'

There was no answer.

'Eli!' Johnny Mac yelled.

No reply.

I walked through the kitchen and into the master bedroom, an addition that had been put on by a previous owner, its location making it easy for midnight snacking. Our private bathroom was attached. I went to the door and knocked. 'Jean?'

'What? I'm taking a bath!' she said, with that 'I'm trying to be patient but you're getting on my last nerve' sound in her voice.

'Eli in there with you?' I asked.

'What? Why would he be?'

'No reason—' I started, but didn't have a chance to finish.

'Milton, don't tell me you've lost Eli!' Jean said, her

voice going into that almost soft tone it gets right before the shit hits the fan.

'I didn't lose him!' I said. 'I just can't find him.'

Turning to my son, I said, 'Come on, Johnny Mac. Let's keep looking.'

Jean was out of the bath, wrapped in a towel and balanced on her crutches in the bathroom doorway before me and Johnny Mac had a chance to get out of the bedroom.

'What happened?' Jean asked.

Without turning to her, I said, 'Gotta keep looking.'

'Milton! What happened?' Jean demanded.

I sighed. 'I don't know! He went out to the car to get his breathie – that's what he calls his inhaler . . .'

'I thought he had it in his pocket,' Jean said.

'He must've forgot it,' I said.

'Did you look in the car for it?' Jean asked.

'It wasn't in there, so he did get in the car and got it.' I said.

'He's around here somewhere. Me and Johnny Mac are gonna find him.'

'I'll get dressed,' Jean said.

'Naw. Just go on and fix some supper. We'll find him.' Turning to my son, I said, 'Let's go, pal.'

Sometimes I'm pretty thick-skulled.

DALTON

'You didn't tell me you was no cop!' Tanjene said, hands on hips, blonde wig slightly askew.

'It didn't come up,' Dalton said. 'You were gonna buy me a cup of coffee?'

Tanjene took her hands off her hips, using her hands to accentuate her words. 'You out of yo' mind? I ain't takin' no cop for coffee! Jeez Louise, you think I'm a idiot?'

'Then could I borrow a couple of dollars?' Dalton asked, blushing.

Tanjene smiled. 'Ah, baby, you so cute when you get all red like that! And no, you cain't borrow no money from me! I work hard for my money, like that ol' song say!'

'Well, thank you for helping me in the alley back there,' Dalton said and started to walk away.

'Oh, now, honey, don't go off in a huff.' She caught up with Dalton and locked arms with him, pressing her ample breasts against his arm. 'I buy you some coffee. I'm sorta off work now anyways.'

They started walking down the street, arm in arm, heading for a coffee shop, when the *wup wup* sound came up behind them. 'Hey, there, Tanjene,' a man said and they both turned around. A Tulsa patrol car was pulled up to the curb, with a uniformed officer hanging out the shotgun side window. 'You got you a paying customer there, Tanjene?'

'No, now honey, he just a friend,' Tanjene said.

Both officers got out of the car and came up onto the sidewalk.

'Ah shit,' Tanjene said under her breath.

'Let's see some ID there, *friend*,' one of the officers said.

'I sorta lost my pants,' Dalton told the officer.

The officer looked down at Dalton's bottom half, 'Then what do you call those?'

Dalton followed the officer's gaze. 'Oh, well, you see—'

'Pat him down, Mike,' the other officer said.

Mike told Dalton, 'Assume the position.'

'Huh?' Dalton said. 'Oh, yeah,' and leaned his hands against the wall of the boarded-up store they were passing.

'Holy shit!' Mike said, coming up with the switchblade. He shoved Dalton hard against the wall, yelling, 'Danny, he's armed!'

Dalton breathed, 'Oh for God's sake.'

HOLLY

Holly was so bored, even her hair hurt. She'd checked out the old barn as much as she possibly could. Besides a rotten-smelling bale of hay in one corner, that's all there was, except, of course, for the props and camera equipment Mr Smith had brought with him. She sure hoped he didn't plan for her to sleep on that cot in this nasty barn. She'd tried climbing up to the hayloft but her hands got dirty on the first rung so she gave that up. Picking out the hay and spitting her hands clean had taken up about an hour, but even that had ended a while ago.

Finally, she heard the muffler of the old van as it turned into the long road toward the barn. She stood outside waiting for it. Mr Smith had barely stepped out of the van before he was waving for her to get back. 'Hurry!' he said. So Holly scooted back into the barn. He came in behind her.

'We start now!' he said, rushing to the video camera on the tripod. He turned it on. 'Stand in front of it, right here,' he marked an 'X' with his foot in the dirt floor. 'Let me get a line on you.' Holly did as she was told. 'OK, now get behind this and film me coming in.' He showed Holly how to work the video camera. 'Here's the scene,' he told her. 'The villain has kidnapped a small child. You are his accomplice. I'll come in and stand on the "X". Make sure the camera is on the "X" and then you come take the child and I'll go back and film. And remember, this kid is a method actor; he's liable to stay in character even when I'm not filming.'

'Really?' said Holly. 'Wow.'

'Get behind the camera!' he said.

'Oh, right. OK, ready. You want me to follow you from when you enter the barn, right?'

'Yes,' Smith said, his teeth clenched.

'Do we need more light?' Holly asked.

'No!' he shouted and headed out to the van.

Holly videotaped as Smith walked in the door carrying a small, squirming bundle wrapped in a blanket. She thought how strange it was that Mr Smith was wearing a bag over his head, but it did have eyeholes cut out. She kept videotaping until he got to the 'X', then, making sure the camera was still running, she ran up to the 'X' to join the other two actors.

'Take him!' Smith shouted, thrusting the still-squirming child into Holly's arms. He ran behind the camera. 'Now, let him out of the blanket!' he said.

Holly carefully lowered her burden to the dirt floor and unrolled the child. That's when she discovered he wasn't squirming for the camera, he was gasping for breath.

Looking up at Smith, she asked, 'Is this method acting or is he dying?'

Smith attempted a laugh. It came out as more of a bark. 'Acting, my dear! What a trooper, eh?'

Looking down at the boy again, she noticed he was trying to say something. 'What?' she said, bending over him.

'Breathie!' he said, gasping for air. 'Breathie!'

Holly shook her head, confused. She had no idea what this kid was saying. She needed a script, damn it!

The boy's hands were tied in front of him, but he managed to point awkwardly toward the front pocket of his blue jeans. Holly felt the outside of the pocket – definitely something in there. She thrust her hand into the pocket and came up with an inhaler.

'What are you doing?' Smith asked, still taping away.

'This kid isn't acting, Mr Smith! He really is having a hard time breathing. Look! He has an inhaler. I think he has asthma or something,' Holly said.

Smith sighed, leaning his head against the coolness of the video camera. This unbalanced the tripod and both it and the video camera hit the dirt floor.

'Here,' Holly said to the boy. 'The camera's off. Let's get these ropes untied and we'll get you your inhaler. Your breathie.'

The child's head nodded vigorously.

MILT

I couldn't find Eli anywhere. Me and Johnny Mac looked all over the backyard, the front yard and in the house – just in case. The boy was gone.

'I can't believe you lost that child!' my wife said.

'I didn't lose him!' I answered. 'He musta run off.'

'Let's get in the car,' Jean said, and we did. We drove her Volvo down the mountain, down both sides, and saw neither hide nor hair of the boy.

Pulling back into the driveway, Jean and I looked at each other, neither saying what we were both thinking.

From the back seat, Johnny Mac asked, 'Where's Eli?'

'Ah—' I started.

Jean cut me off, 'Probably looking for his mommy. Did he say anything to you about wanting to go home?'

'No,' said Johnny Mac, his bottom lip trembling. 'He didn't say nothin' . . .'

'Anything,' Jean corrected automatically.

'We didn't get to play at all!' Johnny Mac cried, bursting into sloppy tears.

We got out of the Volvo and I carried Johnny Mac into the house and handed him over to his mother, then went to the phone to call it in. The kid was gone and there was gonna be hell to pay when I found out who took him.

DALTON

Dalton's first thought was to tell the arresting officers exactly who he was, who he worked for, and beg them to call the sheriff and get him out of this mess. Then he thought of what he'd actually tell the sheriff. How he'd explain the situation. And he realized there was absolutely no way he'd tell anybody in Longbranch what had transpired over the last twenty-four hours. Talk about looking a fool!

'Where's your ID?' asked the sergeant at the city jail desk.

'My pants were stolen,' Dalton explained, looking at the floor, his face already red from the lies he was about to tell.

'Uh huh,' the sergeant said, 'and you just happened to find a pair lying around with a switchblade in the pocket?'

Dalton all but shouted, 'I told you, I took that blade off Tanjene's pimp!'

'Watch it, buddy,' the sergeant said, 'unless you wanna add assaulting an officer to your charges!'

Dalton took a deep breath. 'I'm sorry, sergeant, I didn't mean to yell at you. It's just been a real bad day.'

The sergeant laughed. 'I'll just bet it has. Now, what do you claim your name is?'

'Ah, I'd rather not say,' Dalton answered.

'Excuse me?' the sergeant asked, a sneer on his face.

Blushing, Dalton repeated, 'I'd rather not say.'

'And where do you say you live?' the sergeant asked.

'I'd rather not say.'

Looking at a uniformed officer walking by, the sergeant said, 'Brooks, take this guy to lockup, will ya?'

Dalton began to panic. He'd never been to jail before and he didn't want to start now. 'Ah . . . I get a phone call, right?' he asked. 'One phone call?'

Looking at Officer Brooks, the sergeant nodded his head.

'Come on,' Brooks said, grabbing Dalton's arm and pulling. 'And make it quick, buddy. I don't have all day.'

The only person Dalton could call was the one person in his life who never judged him, never told him what to do and always seemed to listen to him when he needed to talk – his sister, Mary Ellen. It was not common knowledge among the extended family that the antidepressants Mary Ellen had been taking for several years for her chronic clinical depression had numbed her to the point where not only did she not judge other people, she was rarely aware of their existence.

He called her cell phone and, thank the good Lord, she picked up. 'Mary Ellen!' he said. 'I need help!'

'Who is this?' Mary Ellen asked.

'It's . . .' He had started to say 'Dalton', but he saw Officer Brooks standing close enough to hear, so he just said, 'It's your brother.'

'Dalton?' she said.

'Yes!' he said, relieved that she guessed the right one.

'What's the matter?' Mary Ellen asked.

'I'm in jail,' Dalton whispered. 'I need you to come get me out.'

'Let yourself out,' Mary Ellen replied. 'Why are you in your jail? Where are the keys?'

'No!' shouted Dalton in a muted whisper. 'I'm in Tulsa! I'm in *their* jail!'

'Oh,' Mary Ellen said. 'You want me to come get you?' she asked.

'Yes, right away! It's an emergency! Please!' Dalton begged.

'Well, OK, I guess. I can leave in a couple of hours—' she started.

'No!' Dalton interrupted, this time yelling in full voice. He looked around when he realized what he had done and saw everyone – cops and robbers alike – looking straight at him. 'No,' he whispered back to his sister. 'Please, Mary Ellen. Pick me up right away! Leave right this minute!'

On her end of the line, although Dalton couldn't see it, Mary Ellen shrugged. 'OK,' she said. 'I'll leave right now. What's the address?'

MILT

Rodney Knight, Mary Ellen's husband, showed up before any of the authorities, dragging with him his other two children, Rebecca, age eleven, and Rodney, Jr, age two. Mary Ellen had lucked out finding a man taller than her. Seems like a lot of real tall women end up with men shorter than them. Like, if you really measure us, I think I'm like a quarter of an inch shorter than Jean, but since she leans a little on her crutches, you hardly notice. Rodney Knight, though, was like six foot seven or eight, the kind of guy who ducked his head when entering a room. If he weighed 150 pounds, it was because he had on heavy shoes; he was that skinny. He had white-blond hair, the kind that gets a boy called 'Cotton' in my neck of the woods. Don't know if he got called that or not when he was little. Rodney, Jr was a towheaded two-year-old. Cute as a button and full of mischief.

'Is Eli really gone?' Rebecca asked, snapping gum and staring up at me. Damned if she didn't miss the Threepee gene and look like a double of her grandma Clovis! Scrawny for eleven, she had a hooked nose, wore glasses and was more assertive than Threepee and his three kids combined. Definitely Grandma Clovis's clone.

Turning to her father, Rebecca said, 'Daddy, can I have Eli's room?'

Holding two-year-old Junior in his arms, Rodney closed his eyes, appeared to be counting, then said, 'Becca, one more word and you'll go sit in the car.'

'But—' Rebecca started.

'One. More. Word.' Her father said succinctly.

Rebecca mimicked locking her lips and throwing away the key, then leaned up against the wall of our entry hall and began counting the flowers in the wallpaper by poking them sharply with a fingernail.

'Sheriff?' Rodney Knight said, turning toward me.

I shook my head. 'I'm so sorry, Mr Knight. He was with me and Johnny Mac out in the garage, and he just ran out to the car to get his inhaler . . . I just don't know what happened. But I've got the sheriff's department personnel and the Longbranch police personnel on their way up here, and Charlie Smith, the police chief, is staying in town to organize a citizen search party.'

'How long has he been missing?' Eli's father asked me, the baby in his arms squirming as his hold grew tighter. I could see the man trying to relax his grip, but it just wasn't working.

'Jean?' I called to my wife, who was in the kitchen making coffee for the hordes that would soon be descending on us. 'Can you come here a minute?'

When Jean came into the foyer, I smiled. 'Can you take Miss Rebecca here and her little brother up to play with Johnny Mac in the playroom?'

Jean smiled tentatively at Rodney Knight and placed a hand on the arm holding his youngest. 'I'm so sorry this happened, Mr Knight. Please, let me take the kids upstairs.'

He nodded his head and handed over his son.

We watched as the three headed up the stairs, Rebecca taking her baby brother's arm, while my wife negotiated the stairs with one crutch and the stair rail. Rebecca was talking the entire way. 'We can't find Mommy either. I think she ran off with another man. I saw that on TV . . .'

I gestured toward the living room. 'In here?'

He nodded and I followed him in.

'Have you located Mary Ellen?' I asked once we were both seated in the living room.

He shook his head. 'Her cell phone goes directly to voice-mail,' he said. 'I don't know what's going on . . .'

His voice drifted off, as did his gaze, which left me and stared off into space.

I touched his leg, trying to bring him back. 'Is there anyone who would take Eli without permission? I mean, if someone saw him out there without supervision . . .'

Lord, was I feeling guilty about that, but something in the question made Rodney Knight look up. 'Clovis!' he said, standing up. 'She'd do it in a New York minute!'

I stood up too. 'Do you think she has him?' I asked. 'Because if she doesn't, and we called her . . .'

Rodney sat down again. 'I don't even want to think about it,' he said. 'I don't know why she'd be up here, do you?' he asked. 'I mean she doesn't know anyone up here on the mountain.'

'I'll have one of my deputies stop by. Have 'em say they're looking for Dalton . . .'

'Where's Dalton?' Rodney asked, his head jerking up. 'Is he missing, too?'

I couldn't help but think, yeah, actually, he is. Dalton's missing. His nephew's missing. His sister's missing. What's the connection?

'He's been missing since Thursday night,' I told Rodney. 'I doubt if one has anything to do with the other. I think he's with a woman.'

A sad smiled curled Rodney's lips. ''Bout damn time, huh?'

I laughed lightly. 'Yeah, you got *that* right.'

'But Mary Ellen's missing, Dalton's missing and my boy's missing,' Rodney said. 'It has to be connected.'

I shrugged. Three people in one family gone missing in a matter of three days? Yeah, it was suspicious all right. 'Maybe Dalton's not with a woman.'

Rodney's eyes got big. 'Maybe he's not,' he said softly.

FIVE

MARY ELLEN

'I'm here to pick up my brother,' Mary Ellen Pettigrew Knight told the man at the front desk.

'Yeah? Who's your brother?' the man asked.

'Dalton Pettigrew,' she answered.

The man looked at a list in front of him and shook his head. 'We don't have anyone by that name here.'

Mary Ellen stared at the man for a moment, then walked back out the front door.

EMIL

Things aren't going as planned, Emil thought. Who could plan for breaking equipment and a kid with asthma? Nothing he'd found on the Internet about Jean MacDonnell and her family indicated that her son had asthma. As for the broken equipment, he should have looked further than his first interview when he hired an assistant for this gig. Holly Humphries wasn't exactly working out.

'OK, now look into the camera,' he told her. 'Hold up today's newspaper. Tell them how much the ransom is.'

'Wouldn't she cover her face?' Holly asked. 'I mean, she plans to get out of this, right? Why would she let anyone who watched this videotape know her identity?'

He was beginning to hate this girl almost as much as he hated Jean MacDonnell. Glancing down at his feet, he saw the feed sack with the holes cut out for eyes that he had worn when taking the child. He kicked it toward Holly. 'Here,' he said. 'Use this.'

Holly slipped the bag over her head, then immediately tore it off. 'Yuck!' she said. 'This thing stinks!'

No, Emil thought, maybe I hate her a little bit *more* than

Jean MacDonnell! 'Are you an actress or just a wuss?' he demanded.

Holly Humphries stiffened. *She* was an actress. One hundred per cent actress. She reached down to where the feed sack had fallen, picked it up and placed it on her head. With as much dignity as was possible for a young woman wearing a feed sack on her head, Holly said, 'I'm ready when you are, Mr Smith.'

DALTON

It seemed like he'd been in the jail for hours. When he asked Tiny, the oversized man in thong underwear and a wristwatch, what time it was, Dalton discovered he *had* been there for hours. Three, to be exact. So where was Mary Ellen? She should have been there two hours ago.

It took quite a while to get a guard's attention, at least the way Dalton attempted to do it. Finally, Tiny took over, yelling, 'Hey, asshole! Guy needs to talk at'ja!' Which not only got the guard's attention, but his wrath as well.

'What do *you* want?' the little man in the guard's uniform said, looking up at Dalton. 'Trouble? Is trouble what you want? 'Cause I got your trouble right here, pardner!' he said, whacking his left palm with his right hand, which held a billy club.

'No, Sir, not at all.' Dalton attempted a smile. 'I'm just trying to find out—'

'What you smiling at, boy?' the guard said, hitting the bar with the club. 'You coming on to me? You think I'm one a you, asshole? Uh uh, boy. I'm no sissy-pants . . .'

'Leon, what are you doing?' said a tired voice as the head guard came over.

The smaller guard backed away as the older man took his place. The older man sighed. 'You want something, Mr No-Name?'

'I've been waiting for my sister to come get me,' Dalton said. 'Has she been here yet?'

The older guard just stared at him for a minute. Finally,

he asked, 'How is your sister going to find you? We don't have a name for you, stupid.'

As comprehension spread through Dalton's being, tears sprang to his eyes. The realization of exactly what creek he was up finally dawned on him.

SUNDAY

MARY ELLEN

It was the wee hours of the morning and Mary Ellen Pettigrew Knight sat in an all-night coffee shop eating her third piece of pie. This one was pecan. She'd had cherry, chess and now pecan. Mary Ellen Pettigrew Knight had a smile on her face, the first unforced one in three years. She was free – if only for a couple of hours – but she was free. No one knew where she was. No one could get her. No one could make her go home. No children, no husband, no mother.

She was free.

She finished the piece of pie and looked up at the waitress, 'I'm thinking salty. How about some fries?' She was smiling.

MILT

We'd been up all night, all us professionals. I'd finally talked Jean into going to bed around two a.m., but here it was six, and I was still up, searching the creek banks below the falls for the body of Eli Knight. It had been so long now that I knew we were probably looking for a body, not a little boy. Unless a ransom call came in – if the boy was lost, he was probably 100 per cent lost. As in dead.

My cell phone rang and I picked it up. 'Kovak.'

'. . . Jean . . .' came the scratchy voice of my wife. Reception this deep in the woods was not great.

'Hey, babe—' I started but she was already talking.

'. . . call . . . scary . . . ran . . . home . . .'

'Huh?' I said.

'We got . . . man . . . som . . . get . . . now!'

'Baby? We got a bad connection!' I yelled. 'Is it important?'

'Yes!' came back loud and clear. '. . . por . . . now! Ransom!'

The last word rang out like a shot. *Ransom*. Eli Knight might not be dead!

JEAN

Jean wished that she could pace. She envied people who could; it seemed to help with the tension. She sat in the most comfortable chair in the living room, her forearms resting on the arms of the chair, willing them to relax, willing her fists to unclench. Concentrating on the room – as it had been, as it was now. Bachelor digs: a sprung couch with frayed arms, a recliner older than dirt, the TV the dominant feature of the room. Now it was warm, inviting, with good furniture, plants, books, warm colors on the walls. It was their room now, hers and Milt's and John's.

But just thinking John's name brought it all to the forefront. Over and over in her head, she couldn't help replaying the telephone call she'd received only moments before.

That gravelly, mechanical voice. Those words beyond scary: 'I've got your son!' he'd said.

Jean had thrown down the phone and hobbled up the stairs as fast as she could to John's playroom. He was still there, with Dalton's eleven-year-old niece and two-year-old nephew.

She'd gone back downstairs, wondering what the call had been about. Someone saying they had John? But John was upstairs. Eli was missing, not John. Then she had to wonder. Did someone snatch the wrong child? Had someone been after John?

The phone rang again. Jean just stared at it. Finally, she picked it up, 'Hello?'

'Don't hang up on me again!' said the mechanical voice. 'Or your son will pay for it!'

'What do you want?' Jean asked, knowing in her heart that the best thing for Eli Knight right now was for this mechanical-voiced man to continue to think the child he was holding was John Kovak.

'You,' the voice said. 'I want you, Jean.'

MILT

'What does that mean?' I demanded of my wife. 'He wants you?'

Jean shook her head. 'I don't know,' she said, and it was obvious she was trying to hold on to her emotions.

I decided maybe I needed to step up. Maybe I needed to be the calm one here. After all, I was the professional. Just because this seemed to involve my wife and son didn't mean I could act in an unprofessional manner. The hell it didn't. I wanted to scream like a little girl and then strangle the nearest asshole. At this point, any asshole would do.

'He thinks he has *your* son?' Rodney asked.

Jean nodded and sank down into a chair. 'Yes.' She looked up at Eli's father. 'I'm so sorry, Rodney. I'm so sorry your son got caught up in whatever this is.'

Rodney whirled on me. 'Who's after you now, Sheriff?' he said, his voice sounding somewhat mean.

I sank down on the couch. 'I don't know,' I was slightly in shock. 'Can't think who I've pissed off lately.'

'Milt,' my wife said softly. I turned to her.

'Yeah, honey?' I asked, reaching for her hand.

Grabbing mine, she squeezed. 'He didn't ask for you. He knew *my* name. He was talking directly to *me!*'

DALTON

Dalton knew the time was over for keeping this horrible weekend a secret. If he was ever to get out of this place and get home, he had to confess his name.

'Dalton,' he said. 'Dalton Pettigrew.'

'OK, I'll see if anybody's here asking for you.' The older

man turned and walked out of the wing that housed the male prisoners.

The smaller, younger guard waited until the older one left before creeping back to Dalton's cell. 'Nobody coming for you, No-Name,' he said, chuckling. 'You're gonna stay in here until they take you to the funny farm. That's where they take people who don't remember their names. And they lock 'em up and they never let 'em out!'

Dalton straightened up to his full height of six foot, five inches. 'You're a lying sack of shit,' he said to the little man. 'The law clearly states that a person cannot be committed to a mental institution for any more than ninety days unless convicted or sentenced by a judge for a felony offense.'

The little guard stared hard at Dalton, then he broke eye contact and walked away. Tiny slapped Dalton on the back, almost knocking him against the bars. 'Cool!' he said, laughing. 'You got that prick to shut up! First time I *ever* seen that!'

'Thanks!' Dalton said, beaming at Tiny. For some reason, he felt his luck was turning.

MARY ELLEN

Mary Ellen sat in the coffee shop booth, her head resting against the tile wall, sound asleep.

The waitress gently shook her. 'Honey? Honey, you wanna wake up? It's almost six. I don't know what you gotta do today, but I'm thinking you need to wake up.'

Mary Ellen opened one eye. 'I'm sleeping,' she said.

The waitress chuckled. 'Well, I can see that, honey. But you need to get up. Harry – he's the manager –' she said, pointing to the man at the grill, 'he won't let nobody sleep in here. He says it's a hard and fast rule, whatever the hell that means.'

Mary Ellen stretched and looked out the window. Seeing daylight brought her up short. 'Oh, gosh. What time is it?' she asked.

'Six a.m.,' the waitress said. 'Little after that now, 'course, took you so long to get up.' She laughed again and poured Mary Ellen a cup of coffee. 'On the house.'

Mary Ellen thanked her and brought the coffee up to her mouth. Oh, I'm in trouble, she thought. Mama's gonna kill me. But, she had to admit, sitting there with her head propped up against the tile wall was the best sleep she'd had in Lord only knew how long. She sipped at her coffee and sighed. She needed to find Dalton, and she needed to head back home.

MILT

'Any word from your wife?' I asked Rodney.

'No,' he said, his voice short. 'If I hear from her, Sheriff, I'll let you know.'

'Sorry,' I said, 'just asking.'

I could understand the man being peeved. His son was missing, his wife was missing, his brother-in-law was missing – and here I was asking him what must have seemed to him to be stupid questions.

I sighed because of what I had to say next. 'Mr Knight, I'm sorry, but I think we need to call your mother-in-law.'

Rodney Knight jerked his head up from where he'd been changing the diaper of his son. 'Why?'

'Well, for one thing, Eli could be with her; or if not Eli, maybe your wife, or Dalton. If any of them are there, they need to be in on the search. And, well, Sir, your mother-in-law needs to be notified that the second one of her children is missing and one of her grandchildren.'

'Let me call Hawke first,' he said, referring to Dalton's older brother. 'Finish this, would you?' he indicated his son's dirty diaper and took himself and his cell phone into the other room.

I stood there looking at Rodney, Jr, and his poop. It had been a short eighteen months since I'd had to change my own son, and this just didn't seem fair. I'd done my duty – excuse the expression. Rodney, Jr looked up at me and giggled. He seemed to be enjoying my discomfort.

I leaned down and grabbed a wipie and went to work.

'Just remember,' I told Rodney, Jr, 'I might still be sheriff when you turn driving age. And, boy-hidy, watch out.'

He seemed to find this amusing and laughed out loud. 'I'm not kidding,' I told him. 'I'm dead serious here. Gonna throw your hiney in jail!'

This, to my chagrin, seemed to be hysterically funny. 'You're not taking me seriously here, Rodney, Jr!'

I finished, picked him up and placed his feet on the floor, just as his father came in from the dining room.

'I talked to Hawke. He was at his mother's this morning. No one was there but her. He didn't know anything about Eli or Mary Ellen. Hawke's gonna go see Chief Smith in town. See what he can do to help on that end. He didn't know about Dalton, either, for that matter. Until Clovis told him. He says she's still very upset about Dalton. Thinks it's all your fault,' he said, raising his head to look me dead in the eye, the look seeming to say, 'Like everything else is your fault!'

Hell, I knew losing that child was my fault. How in the hell I ended up letting a four-year-old walk out to the car by himself, I didn't hardly know. It made me sick at my stomach that the child was gone, and made me sicker still knowing I was to blame. I looked at Eli's little brother, now in his daddy's arms, and wondered if this baby would ever know his big brother Eli.

Oh, yeah. He'd know him all right. Time, I decided, to get my ass in gear.

EMIL

He'd heard her voice and it had all come rushing back. He'd remembered the facts, remembered everything from almost the moment he woke up. But now he also remembered the feelings she brought out in him. At first, it had just been the need to manipulate the cripple. Take advantage of the vulnerable. But Jean MacDonnell hadn't been as vulnerable as he had thought. At first he was sure he was getting to her – his authority over her, his God-like control made her as vulnerable as any of his other interns. And the fact that she was older made the conquest of her all the more desirable. But she'd turned on him before he'd even had a go at her.

How dare she treat him like that! He wasn't 'God-like', damn it, he *was* God! Her God, all his interns' God! The rest of them knew – why didn't she? How dare she question him? How dare she go to the 'authorities' over him? *No one* had authority over him! He was Emil Hawthorne! He *was* the authority! *He* was God!

Now she would know how it felt to have something wonderful and special taken from her. He had taken her son, just as she had taken his power. Stolen it away from him, betrayed him for some silly moral code! Thinking ethics and morals were of higher value than him. Well, she'll find out, he thought. She'll find out what ethical and moral codes she'll break to get her son back!

HOLLY

Holly sat beside the little boy, holding his hand as he inhaled deeply from his 'breathie'.

'You feeling better?' she asked.

He nodded his head.

'What's your name?' Holly smiled at him.

'Eli,' he answered.

She held out her hand, 'I'm Holly.'

Eli shook her hand and said, 'Nice to meet you.'

Holly grinned. 'Goodness, you are a polite young man.'

'Yes, I am,' Eli replied.

Holly ruffled his hair and got up from the cot, walking over to where Mr Smith sat, staring at the camera equipment.

'Eli's feeling better,' she told him.

It took a beat, then Mr. Smith turned to her. 'Who?' he asked.

'Eli,' she gestured behind her to where Eli sat on the cot, his inhaler in hand.

'His name's John,' Mr Smith said.

'Huh?' Holly started and then nodded her head. 'Oh, right. In the story. Sorry, I didn't know.'

Mr Smith stood up and stared at her. 'No, in life. His name is John.'

Confused, Holly said, 'Then Eli is his story name?'

Mr Smith rushed over to the cot and grabbed the boy, lifting him up by both arms. 'What's your name?' he yelled in the boy's face.

The boy began to cry and Holly pulled at Mr Smith's arm, grabbing the boy away from him. 'Stop that!' she yelled at her benefactor.

Holly sank down onto the cot with her arms around Eli, cradling him against her.

Mr Smith breathed in deeply, counting to ten. Attempting a smile, he said to the boy, 'I'm sorry. Could you tell me your name, please?'

The little boy removed the thumb that had gone into his mouth, and said shyly, 'Eli Thomas Knight.'

Holly was mystified when Mr Smith fell to the floor, covered his face with both hands and began to weep.

MILT

'I didn't let him know he had the wrong child,' my wife said. 'I thought it would be safer for Eli if this animal thought he had John.'

Jean calls our boy 'John'. I call him 'Johnny Mac'. It probably confuses him, but it works for me and Jean. His whole name is John MacDonnell Kovak, but I think Johnny Mac Kovak has a certain ring to it. If he wants to be a doctor or a lawyer or a CPA when he grows up, John MacDonnell Kovak will look fine on his door; but if he wants to be just cool, what could be better than Johnny Mac Kovak? '*And on guitar, Johnny Mac Kovak . . .*', '*And playing right field, Johnny Mac Kovak . . .*' See how that works?

'Probably the right call,' I told her, putting my hand on her shoulder. 'If Johnny Mac's who he was going for, best he keep thinking that's who he's got.'

'Sheriff, I want my son back!' Rodney Knight suddenly announced, still holding his other son in his arms. The boy was squirming fit to beat the band, but Rodney, Sr wasn't letting go.

'Yes, Sir, I want him back, too. And we're working toward that.' To prove that point, I picked up my cell phone and called the office. Gladys answered the phone; she'd come in on her day off due to the missing child.

'Sheriff's office,' she said.

'Get any reports in?'

'Don't you think I'd call you if I heard anything?' she said, all snippy like she gets.

'Do I need to come down there?' I asked her, my dander up.

'What? You gonna put me in time out or spank me?'

I grinned. 'You know, I could put you up on charges for sexual harassment now?'

I could practically hear her blushing over the phone once she figured out the implications of what she'd just said. Finally, she said, 'That's not what I meant!'

'Where is everybody?' I asked, basically ignoring her.

'Emmett's down in the south quadrant checking those old trailers down there, Anthony and some of Charlie Smith's people are dividing up the Bishop area and I got another civilian search party being led by Lonnie doing the northeast quadrant.'

Lonnie Sturgis was our weekend deputy who mainly just looked after the jail, but he was good at leading civilian search parties, as had been proven about a year ago when a couple from the old folks home disappeared. Lonnie and some of his volunteers found them after two days, still alive in their old car deep in a gully off a side road in the far east of the county. It had been a miracle, and Lonnie was a hero for a while after that. Every dog should have its day, I always say. Well, I think it sometimes, anyway.

'OK,' I told Gladys, 'let's call 'em back in. Seems we got a ransom demand. I think maybe the boy's been kidnapped instead of just being lost.'

'How in the world did that happen?' Gladys demanded.

Stiffening, as the guilty often do, I said, 'Let's just concentrate on getting the boy back, shall we?'

HOLLY HUMPHRIES

Holly felt scared watching Mr Smith cry. She wasn't used to seeing older men cry. Young ones, sure. She had a boyfriend once who used to cry watching TV commercials, but an old guy, no, she wasn't used to that. Holly wasn't much of a crier herself. She figured with the life she'd had up to now, if she ever started crying, she might never stop.

Holly had been five years old when her mother told her she wasn't going to be able to keep her any more. 'It's just too hard,' she had said, always one to be absolutely truthful with her small child whenever it suited her purpose. 'I can't save any money when I have to pay childcare. And it's hard to buy food, what with the childcare, and you keep growing out of your clothes. It's just a real expense, Holly, and I just don't make that kind of money.'

So Holly had gone with her mother to a big building in Tulsa, where she'd sat on a chair, her Hello Kitty bag next to her filled with socks and underwear and two outfits and four toys: all her mother said she could bring with her ('I'll give the rest of it to the poor children who don't have anything,' Holly's mother had told her), and watched her mother sign her young life away.

She'd spent that night, plus the next six, at a halfway house, where she lost all but one toy to the other children who'd grabbed them the minute she walked in. She kept her stuffed dog in her panties so that no one could get it. She peed on it once when she went to the bathroom, but she was very good about cleaning it thoroughly in the sink. It was cold and wet after that for quite a while, and it began to stink not long after.

Her first actual placement was at a foster home with two 'reals' and four 'fosters'. She'd been the youngest. The 'mother' was real nice, but the 'father' never did anything but yell. Most of the kids ignored her, except for the youngest 'real', who took an instant dislike to this usurper of the 'baby' position. She did things like flush stuff down the toilet and tell her mother that Holly had done it, cut up Holly's only clothes and again blame it on Holly, saying Holly told her she was going to trick the 'mother' into buying her a whole new wardrobe. Holly's punishment for that was wearing the same outfit every day for two weeks. It was her responsibility to wash it every night. Her preschool teacher called child welfare about that, and Holly was moved again.

By the time she 'aged out' at eighteen, Holly had been in six foster homes and three halfway houses. She'd been molested by an older 'brother' when she was twelve, beaten up by an older 'sister' when she was fifteen, and ran away and ended up in juvie for two days when she was sixteen.

Throughout all of this, Holly had kept an active fantasy life, shutting out much of what was actually happening to her. It was inevitable that she would navigate toward the theater, since theater had been her entire life. You want a little girl who smiles and says 'Thank you'? You got it. You want a little girl who tells jokes and acts sassy? Got it right here. You want a little girl who sits on your lap and ignores the hard thing poking her leg? No problem. Holly was not a born actress, but a bred one. She just wanted to start getting paid for it.

But in all those years, she'd never seen one of her foster fathers cry, nor one of the men at any of the halfway houses. She thought older men just didn't cry, until Mr Smith started bawling his eyes out.

But it was a lot scarier when Mr Smith *stopped* crying.

Awkwardly, he got to his feet, his eyes never leaving the boy's face. Holly didn't like the way Mr Smith was looking at him. Her arms instinctively tightened around the child in her lap.

'Who are you?' he asked the boy, his voice soft and more frightening still.

The child clung to Holly. 'Mr Smith,' she said, 'you're scaring him.'

'Where's John Kovak?' Mr Smith demanded.

Eli looked up at Holly, confusion clouding his face, and then looked back at Mr Smith. 'At his house?' the boy answered.

'I thought that's where I got you,' Mr Smith said. 'At John Kovak's house.'

Eli nodded his head. 'Yes, Sir,' he said. 'Me and John was gonna play,' he said, then clouded up and began to cry again.

'Stop that!' Mr Smith roared, which only made the child cry harder.

Holly picked up the boy in her arms and stood up, his head on her shoulder. 'You leave him alone!' she said, indignantly. 'You're not a very good director, Mr Smith!'

Holly wasn't sure whether it was before or after Mr Smith began to tie up her and the boy that she finally decided he wasn't a movie director after all. She decided there was something not quite kosher about this whole experience. It was also around this time that Holly decided she needed to get herself and the child out of the barn. If not, they were both going to be in very deep shit.

DALTON

'Mary Ellen!' Dalton said, relief pouring through him as he came out of the door that led from the cells to the real world. He saw his sister, all six feet of her, standing at the desk, hunched over as always, awaiting his release.

Mary Ellen gave her little brother a finger wave. 'Hey, Dalton,' she said.

Dalton came up and threw his arms around her, hugging her tightly. Mary Ellen just stood there, arms at her sides, as the hug continued.

Backing away, Dalton grinned one of his huge grins. 'Boy, am I glad to see you. And you can bet I'm ready to head home!' He put his arm around his sister's shoulders. 'Let's get out of here!'

It was proof of Dalton's hard weekend that he didn't notice his sister said nothing about his strange pants or lack of shoes, something the Mary Ellen of old would have jumped on in a New York minute.

Mary Ellen led the way to her minivan and got behind the wheel. As she started up the van and headed out of the parking lot, Dalton reached for her cell phone, sitting on the bench seat between them. 'I'm gonna call Mama—' Dalton started, but Mary Ellen grabbed the cell phone and threw it out the window. The sound of the phone smashing to bits was music to her ears.

'Gee, Mary Ellen, why'd you do that?' Dalton asked, truly confused.

'I'm not ready to go home yet,' Mary Ellen said, still staring straight ahead.

'Ah, I think my car's parked back that way,' Dalton said, pointing in the opposite direction from where they were headed.

'Oh?' Mary Ellen said. She shook her head. 'Road trip!'

MILT

Charlie Smith, having an actual budget for his Longbranch Police Department, was able to come over to my house with telephones and tracing equipment. We weren't ready to call in the FBI, since we'd never actually gotten a ransom demand, per se. We were on our own, but Charlie and his department would be a big help.

We set up all the equipment in the living room and sat Jean in front of the main phone.

'Why don't I answer the phone?' Rodney Knight demanded. 'It's my son!'

'But he thinks he has Johnny Mac,' I reminded him. 'And he said he wanted Jean. She needs to answer the phone.'

Having been relieved of his two-year-old by one of the volunteers, he threw up his hands in exasperation and began pacing the living room.

Charlie and I moved off into a corner. 'Who you think this guy is?' Charlie asked.

I shook my head. 'I've got no earthly idea.'

'Think Jean does?'

I resented the implication, but looked over at my wife anyway. Damn it to hell if she didn't look guilty of something. Of course, I was feeling all kinds of guilty letting the boy go out to the car by himself; maybe that's the kind of guilt Jean was feeling. But looking at her, I sort of doubted it.

'I'll get back with you,' I told Charlie. I left him standing there while I went to sit on the couch as close to my wife as I could get.

'How you doing?' I asked her.

Jean nodded her head, then said, 'OK, I guess. Tense.'

'Yeah,' I agreed, 'tense situation. Why do you think that guy said he wanted you? You got any idea why someone would want to take our child, honey?'

Tears sprang to her eyes. 'Yes,' she said quietly.

PART II
JEAN'S STORY

SIX

JEAN'S STORY

Where do I start my story? When I first met him? Or why he wanted me in the first place? That goes back a ways – to when I was two years old. That's when the Salk vaccine came out. My father, a biologist, had known Dr Salk briefly and disliked him intensely, which is the reason he refused my mother's request to have her six children vaccinated. I was the youngest, and the only one to contract polio.

Like I said, I was only two, and I do believe my subconscious blocked out most of that time, as I have no memory of any of it. Only the aftermath – all the painful physical therapy to try to stretch out my left leg, all the therapy baths that were supposed to help – so many that, to this day, I can't get in a Jacuzzi. Then the braces on my leg, the crutches that had to grow with me – new ones every six months or so. Who knew a little girl could grow so fast?

And then there was school. Thank God I had a best friend who went everywhere with me, including to school. I don't think I would have made it without Rene. She may not have been visible to my parents, teachers or classmates, but she was very real to me. Rene was the one who'd have a witty comeback every time some child said something hurtful. She would protect me from being cut by their words by slinging the words back, twisted and shaped into something special just for that child.

Unfortunately, Rene went away around my freshman year in high school, leaving me basically defenseless. Every time a teacher would tell my parents that I was far above grade level, I'd beg them to let me go on, to be where I should be intellectually – to hell with chronology. This being the early seventies, and having only the current information *available to them, they agreed. I made it through high school in two years, graduating at the age of fifteen. I managed to graduate mid-term, so there was no ceremony, no crossing a stage on crutches to the laughter of my fellow students. Unbeknownst to them, I had won.*

Because of my shortened high school career and an accelerated program as an undergrad, I went into the doctorate program at the University of Chicago at nineteen, having no idea what I wanted to be when I grew up.

To make what turned out to be a very long story short, I was the oldest intern in my program when I finally finished medical school – having already received one PhD in philosophy, one in English literature and one in biophysics – a discipline I actually worked in for four years.

As an intern, I did OK in most of my rotations and had almost picked a specialty in the psych rotation when it was my time. That's where I met him – Emil Hawthorne, MD. He was chair of the department, even had a wing of the hospital named after him. He wasn't an attending – there were several lesser souls for that; he was the guru, for want of a better word, our Svengali, Machiavelli or, for those in need of more modern historical references, our Charles Manson, Jim Jones, David Koresh.

He was brilliant; there was no getting around that. A brilliant, brilliant man. And in his own way, he was quite attractive. Slightly shorter than my five feet, ten inches, he was slight of build, with abundant dark hair falling below his collar. And his eyes. I'm sure Svengali and Machiavelli had eyes like that. Maybe not the deep, almost night-sky blue, or even the exotic almond shape, but the way they could capture you, keep you suspended in time and space, make you forget what you were saying or thinking, only leave you to remember what you were feeling, and those feelings always came back to those eyes, those mesmerizing eyes.

Did I do what I did because I was jealous? I've asked myself that a thousand times. Or did I do what I did because it was the right, the moral thing to do? Who knows? But I did it. Which is all that counts now. And because I did it, he tried to take my son. The fact that he didn't succeed, took another child instead, didn't diminish my guilt or my shame. A child was in harm's way because of me.

DALTON

'Mary Ellen,' Dalton said, a slight whine in his voice, 'I don't understand. Where are we going? I really need to get my car and go home! I'm super tired!'

'Then close your eyes,' Mary Ellen said, a dreamy smile on her face. 'I'll wake you when we get there.'

'Get *where*?' Dalton demanded.

The smile grew. 'You'll see.'

HOLLY

Holly Humphries had decided that this entire thing was a hoax and there was no movie. It had taken her a while, as she had been fairly deep in denial, a place where Holly was quite comfortable. After all, Holly did claim to be an actress, although at the age of twenty-three she'd had fourteen jobs, and not one of them – until Mr Smith – had been an actual paying acting gig. She'd worked at a video store, a supermarket, a dry cleaners, Wal-Mart, a multiplex movie theater (where she got fired for watching the movies instead of working), McDonald's, Dollar General and several more stores, all for minimum wage. At one point, a friend told her that the city was hiring workers at the waste water treatment plant and training them, and that they were looking for women because they didn't have any and were supposed to have some. *And* they were paying big bucks just for the training! So Holly signed up for the training program and lasted long enough to find out what waste water actually was.

Her highest paying job was at an adult video and book store. Unfortunately, she never got a paycheck because she lasted less than a day. When the first customer came to her counter with a video featuring a picture of a naked, big-busted woman tied down with chains, Holly took the opportunity to inform him that he was a creep and could use some intense counseling. The management felt her customer relations were less than what they sought. She was asked to leave.

But as much in denial as she might have been, the realization finally came to Holly. Mr Smith was up to something other than making a movie, and somehow it involved this poor little boy. Like maybe a kidnapping or something. There was only one person here to save him: Holly Humphries. She could see the headlines in the Tulsa paper now: 'Young Actress saves Child from Demented Psycho,' 'Kidnapping Scheme Foiled by Holly Humphries, Actress (Résumé on Page 6)'.

Unfortunately, her heroic exploits were thwarted by the fact that both she and the boy were tied up. But the dampness of the old barn was getting to Eli, and his breathing became raspy again.

'Mr Smith!' Holly called out to the man sitting dejectedly at a table halfway across the barn. 'He needs his inhaler again!' When he didn't reply, she said 'Mr Smith, please! He can't breathe!'

Finally 'Mr Smith' turned around, saw the inhaler on the table and picked it up, tossing it to the girl.

'His hands are tied, Mr Smith! Please!' she said, exaggerating her agitation. *Acting* the part of a helpless victim.

'Mr Smith' got up, walked over to where the 'breathie' lay on the ground and picked it up. He took it to the child and roughly pushed him over, untying his wrists from behind his back. 'Here,' Mr Smith said, 'breathe.'

He shoved the 'breathie' at the boy and walked off. Holly leaned down and whispered to Eli, 'Use your breathie, then untie my hands, OK?'

He nodded his head, inhaling deeply. After two deep breaths, he stuck the inhaler in his pocket and, looking for 'Mr Smith', and finding him with his back to his victims, began to quietly untie Holly Humphries's hands.

JEAN'S STORY

I'd only been in the psych rotation for a couple of weeks when I was hand-picked to be Dr Hawthorne's personal intern. I'd never been on a rotation where the head of the department had a 'personal intern', but this was psychiatry and would be different by its very nature. And so, I began my relationship with Emil Hawthorne.

I had avoided relationships of any kind for most of my life, which was one of the reasons I stayed in school for so long, getting degree after degree. Not going into the real world kept me from having to face a real life. So at this late age it was only enviable that I would fall – and fall hard. I did anything he asked of me without question. Where a regular intern might work twelve to eighteen hours a day, I'd work around the clock, catching catnaps where I could, showering at the hospital, keeping a change of clothes readily available. One of those changes of clothes was a little black dress, ready for the moment that Dr Hawthorne turned around, really saw me for the first time and said, with a catch in his voice, 'Dr MacDonnell, would you have dinner with me, please?'

Looking back, I know that I was too naïve to realize what was happening, even though I was almost a decade older than the other interns. I didn't understand that the late nights, the exhaustion, the subtle touches to my hand or arm, the secret smiles just for me, were all part of the seduction. That the seduction itself was the goal, and that sex had very little to do with it.

Then one day Greta showed up – a terribly thin, blonde woman with a German accent, his personal intern from the previous semester. I didn't meet her, I only saw her going into his office. One of the other interns, still on rotation from the semester before, offered up the girl on a plate to the other interns standing there, not realizing I was nearby.

'Oh, yeah,' he said, a smirk on his face. 'That's Greta. Dr Hawthorne's personal intern last year, if you know what I mean.' From the sound of the laughter there was no doubt that everyone knew what he meant. 'I heard she had to leave the program.' He shrugged his shoulders.

'*Don't know why. But you know that old saying, never shit where you eat.'*

'*Oh, gross,' one of the women said, and everyone laughed again.*

As the others wandered off, I maneuvered myself to see in through the glass door of Dr Hawthorne's office. Greta, the former intern, or whatever she was, was standing in front of Emil Hawthorne, both hands clinging to his arm, her posture obviously that of someone begging for something. Tears were running down her face. The look on Hawthorne's face froze me. A mixture of obvious ingredients: disgust, pity and, most telling and most terrifying, triumph.

I won't deny that I was a woman obsessed. Although the obsession changed, the object of that obsession didn't: I was still out to get Emil Hawthorne, but not as a dinner companion or possible future lover. The look on his face as Greta begged him for whatever it was she wanted had awakened – and disgusted – me. It was at that moment that I realized there was something wrong with Emil Hawthorne, something terribly wrong. But no one seemed to see it except for me. It became my responsibility to stop him.

Over the next week, and only at night after Dr Hawthorne had gone home for the day, leaving me a stack of work that could break a lesser being's spirit if not back, I would sneak into the intern records, looking for the people who had served as Dr Hawthorne's 'personal intern' over the years. Going back two and a half years, I found five. All were female. One had a speech impediment, one had a weight problem, one was in a wheelchair and one had a prosthetic arm. Only Greta had no apparent handicap. Until I found her psych eval.

Every intern going into a psych rotation had to take a psychological evaluation. I did; everyone else did, too. As did Greta Schwartzmann Nichols. Although Greta had been born and raised, for the most part, in Germany, there were records available. And I discovered Greta's handicap was not something one could see, like a wheelchair, crutches or a prosthetic arm, or something one could hear, like a speech impediment. Greta's handicap was severe physical abuse by her father. Five broken bones by the age of six, removal from the home twice. But each time Greta and her siblings were returned to their home – that is, until their father killed Greta's younger brother. Then she and her sister were taken away for good and given over to the state.

An American Air Force officer and her husband adopted both girls and brought them back to the States. But by this time, Greta was sixteen, and the damage of her father's attentions and the attentions of men in the system supposedly designed to care for children of the state, had done their damage. I think it's safe to say that Greta Schwartzmann Nichols was the most vulnerable of Emil Hawthorne's 'personal interns'.

I was lucky that I found out about Dr Hawthorne's penchant for 'damaged' female interns before I became one of them. I was repulsed by what I found out, but I also knew there was nothing legally wrong with what he was doing. I'm sure there was some statute on the books at the teaching hospital explaining that fraternizing with interns was a no-no, but the most the eminent Dr Hawthorne would get was a slap on the wrist.

But as I sat there looking at the file for Greta Schwartzmann Nichols, I couldn't help thinking that if he preferred damaged and vulnerable young women, the best pool of applicants would not be his interns – it would be his patients.

EMIL

In a funk, Emil sat on a bale of hay, staring at his reflection in the dull gleam of the van he'd used to kidnap the boy. How could he have gotten the wrong boy? How could this have happened? What kind of luck did he have that this . . .

And then it dawned on him. It wasn't bad luck at all. It was Jean MacDonnell. She did it to him again. And now she was laughing at him. She'd gleefully handed him the wrong child, and now she was sitting up there in her house

on that silly hill they call a mountain around here, laughing
at him.

But he had an idea that would turn her smile upside down.
How funny would it be – hilarious, really – for her to find
this little changeling she'd given him in pieces on her front
steps?

HOLLY

Holly tried not to get antsy – after all, Eli was just a baby,
really. He couldn't help it that he was having a hard time
untying her restraints. But she also couldn't help herself.
'Hurry!' she urged in a whisper.

Which, of course, stopped the four-year-old in his tracks.
'I can't!' he whined.

'Shhh!' Holly said, then quickly cooed, 'It's OK, Eli. It's
OK. Just do the best you can so we can get away from
here, OK?'

He nodded his head and rubbed his dripping nose on his
sleeve, then set back to work, trying to untie the rope from
Holly's wrists.

DALTON

Dalton woke up to silence. Well, not exactly silence. He
could hear birds cooing, wind whispering through tree
branches, but no engine noise. The minivan was stopped, and
he was alone. Dalton was sitting in the shotgun seat, which
had been put in the reclining position. He found the handle
to bring the seat back up, lifted it and tried to orient himself.
He had no idea where his sister was. The driver's side door
was open, which meant the overhead light should be on, but
it wasn't. He saw that the keys were in the ignition. He fina-
gled himself into the driver's seat and turned the key.

Nothing happened. Just the *click – click –* of a dead
battery. Where was Mary Ellen and how long had she been
gone? Dalton figured it must have been for a while if the open
door was able to have killed the battery, unless the battery
was already in bad shape. Had Mary Ellen mentioned a bad

battery? He tried to remember, then he realized Mary Ellen hadn't told him much of anything lately.

He got out of his sister's minivan and looked around. He had no idea where he was. A dirt road in the middle of nowhere, lots of tall trees and that appeared to be that. Finally, he cupped his hands around his mouth, making a small megaphone, and called out, 'Mary Ellen!' as loud as he could. There was no response.

Dalton looked up at the star-studded sky, thinking it had only been yesterday – or was it the day before – not long ago, that he'd wished upon these very stars, wished that he and his Sarah would live a happy life.

God, what a joke, he thought bitterly. Him and his Sarah. Ah, change that to Geoffrey, please. How could he be such an idiot? To think that a girl as lovely as that one *appeared* to be would want him? That any girl would want him! He held his head up to the sky again, and resigned himself to a life lived in solitude.

MARY ELLEN

Mary Ellen sat on a rock, watching the water fall into the pool below. She'd come as far as she could. The one place she remembered being happy: Mountain Falls.

She and Rodney used to come here when they were in high school, sit in the front seat of the car and listen to the radio, to Huey Lewis and the News, Boy George, Cyndi Lauper. They would kiss and touch but never go too far. Mostly, they'd just hold each other and stare at the water-fall, making plans for their life together.

She wasn't sure when it went bad or why. But she really hadn't felt that good since Rodney, Jr was born. It had been a hard birth; she'd bled a lot and had to have transfusions. She hadn't been able to breastfeed her baby, as she'd been too sick and dehydrated. She felt she never bonded with Rodney, Jr the way she had with the other two. She also felt that her bond with those first two children was slipping. As was the bond with her husband. Things weren't right and she didn't know why.

Maybe this was the end of the trail. The dead end. Nothing forward except the cliff that could take her flying into the pool below. The thought of flying made her smile. She'd had a dream once that she was flying. It was the best dream she'd ever had, and, try as she might, she never could get it to come back. In the dream she was trying to catch something, or somebody, but they were going too fast, and she was running, running, running, trying to catch up, but her feet were going too slow for the rest of her. Finally, she just picked them up – her feet – and off she went, flying after whatever it was she wanted. Then, of course, as dreams tend to do, it switched and she was no longer after anyone, just flying for the sake of flying. It was a wonderful feeling, full of joy and wonder, even if she didn't get very far off the ground. Hey, it was *her* dream, and she could stay *almost* grounded as much as she wanted.

She looked out over the night-filled pool below, as it reflected the little light given off by the moon, wondering if she could fly again, this time for real. Just let go and swoop down into the pool like an eagle or a hawk, fly off, following the stream of Mountain Falls Creek as it moved on to wherever it went, maybe to the Red River, even, or on into Texas. Maybe as far as the Gulf of Mexico.

But then from nowhere came a voice: 'But what about your babies?' it asked.

'Shhh,' Mary Ellen said into the silent night. 'Shhh . . .'

JEAN'S STORY

It proved more difficult getting into patient records than it had getting into intern records. Actually, it was fairly close to impossible. It took a week of planning and sweet-talking a motherly nurse (which, ironically, was very close to what I was accusing Emil Hawthorne of), but I managed to get my hands on a year's worth of his patients' records. I knew I was breaking the law, risking my medical license, and I'm not sure if I was really doing it because of his past and future victims, or if I was just pissed off that he had intended for me to be one of them – maybe I was just seeking my own kind of revenge.

Knowing what I did about him, it didn't take long to pick out his potential victims: women under the age of thirty, with a physical, emotional or psychological handicap. There were five of them in the past year, two of them current patients. That meant three who might be willing to talk to me.

Since I was working close to twenty-four hours a day, it was hard to get the time off, but a nice phony cough got me off the floor and home, supposedly in bed. I'd made copies of the files; the first was Melinda Hayes, a twenty-seven-year-old market analyst who worked at a brokerage house downtown. She was physically fine, but she had spent five years of her life on the run in Mexico with a father who had kidnapped her from her mother's custody. It hadn't been a good five years.

She agreed to see me at her office on the twenty-first floor of one of the taller buildings in downtown Chicago. The twenty-first floor was all her company, and if it wouldn't have been overly ostentatious, I'm sure they would have papered the walls in gold. The reception area was full of actual antiques, oriental rugs over mahogany floors, and it screamed good taste.

I was greeted by the receptionist, who then called a secretary, who, in turn, took me to Ms Hayes's office. Both of these women were my age, but they could easily have been runway models, they were that gorgeous.

But when I saw Melinda Hayes, the beauty of the other two women faded. She was of obvious mixed race, with beautiful café-au-lait skin, light brown hair pulled back in a French braid, almond-shaped eyes of piercing blue, full lips and a perfectly shaped, hourglass body.

She held out her hand to me, nails perfectly done, and said, 'Dr MacDonald, is it?'

'MacDonnell,' I corrected, smiling. 'Thank you for seeing me, Ms Hayes.'

'Please, have a seat,' she said, indicating one of two silk damask-covered side chairs. I took one and she took the

other. 'I must say, I'm curious. You mentioned Dr
Hawthorne?'

'Yes,' I said, *treading carefully.* 'I'm on his service at the
hospital.'

*The second model I'd seen earlier, the secretary, stuck
her head in the door.* 'Melinda, may I get you and your
guest some refreshments?'

*Melinda Hayes arched an eyebrow at me in question, and
I shook my head. Looking back at the door, I smiled and
said,* 'No, thank you.'

'I'm fine, Angela, thank you,' *Melinda said, sending the
young woman on her way.*

Turning back to me, Melinda Hayes said, 'I'm curious
how my name came up and why you're here.'

'Just going over old patient files,' *I lied,* 'to see if there's
any need for follow-up.'

Melinda Hayes laughed. 'Is Emil that hard up for patients
these days?'

'No, of course not,' *I said, also laughing.* 'But do you
think this would work if he was?'

Her laughter faded. 'I suppose it would depend on the
patient,' *she said and stood up.* 'Thank you for dropping
by, although I can't see why this wasn't done by phone call.
"No" is so much easier over the phone.'

'Exactly why I'm here in person,' *I said, also standing,
but smiling at her.*

The smile she returned to me wasn't the friendliest. 'Yes,
I suppose so,' *she said, walking toward the door. Opening
it, she called out,* 'Angela!'

The secretary came running, a tight smile on her face.
'Yes, Melinda?'

'Please see my guest out.' *Turning to me, she stuck out her
hand.* 'So nice to meet you. Please tell your Dr Hawthorne
to never contact me again.'

*With that, she turned abruptly and went back into her
office, slamming the door behind her.*

Angela turned toward me and gave me a contrite smile.
'Sorry,' *she said, leading me toward the elevator.* 'She gets
that way sometimes.'

'I hope I didn't upset her,' I said.

'Doesn't take much,' Angela replied, almost under her breath.

I lowered my voice as I said, 'Hard to work for, eh?'

'You don't know the half of it!' Angela whispered back.

Putting my future as a physician at risk, I took a gulp of air and asked, 'May I buy you a cup of coffee?'

EMIL

Emil Hawthorne was still sitting on his bale of hay, feeling sorry for himself. He didn't stir until he heard a commotion at the back of the barn. He turned, just in time to see Holly Humphries's backside slipping out a hole in the back wall of the barn. The kid was nowhere in sight.

'Jesus H Christ on a bicycle!' Emil said, standing up and running to the back of the barn. 'Holly!' he screamed through the hole. 'Holly! You get back here! And bring that brat with you! Holly!'

Abruptly, he sat down on the barn's dirt floor and thought seriously about crying again. He took a deep breath of air, pulled his cell phone out of his pocket and dialed. When someone answered, he said, 'Things aren't going so well.'

HOLLY

Holly had no idea where she was. She was a Tulsa-born city girl, and didn't know diddly about the woods. And now, she was deep in them. She wished, for the first time in her life, that she'd paid attention the one time she went to a Camp Fire Girls meeting; maybe now she'd know which way was north. Not that she had any idea which direction Tulsa might be.

After aging out of the foster care system, Holly had stayed in Tulsa, the only town she had ever known, and initially moved in with three girls she knew through the system, one of whom left crack vials in the living room, and one who had a different guy spending the night every night. Holly and the third girl, Vivian, left after one such boyfriend tried to climb into bed with Vivian. The two got a very small efficiency apartment where they were able to live for almost six months, until Holly came home from one of her minimum-wage jobs to find a note from Vivian saying she'd decided to move to Dallas to find her father.

Holly wished her well but ended up bunking on someone's couch after her rent ran out on the efficiency apartment. She crashed on this couch until she met and moved in with the love of her life, Joshua. Joshua was a musician and didn't have a last name, so Holly signed the lease on a one-bedroom apartment, the most space Holly had ever lived in without a foster parent or halfway house director.

Holly stuck with her minimum-wage jobs, since Joshua wasn't yet making much money as a musician. Actually, he played for free most of the time – really, all the time – but he couldn't hold down a job because his gigs kept him up until the wee hours of the morning, and how could he hold down a job like that? So Holly took on a second minimum-wage job to pay the rent on the one bedroom. There were months when they went without electricity and water because she couldn't pay the bill, and often they would eat nothing but whatever leftovers Joshua brought home from the bars where he played for free. But Holly was in love and knew that one day Joshua would be a big star and she would live in a mansion and would be able to take acting lessons and maybe make her own movie.

Then one day she came home at her usual time from her earlier job to find Joshua in bed with another man. When she made a commotion about it, both Joshua and the other man suggested she join them. Holly packed her two bags' worth of belongings and ended up on someone else's couch. Again. She'd heard the landlord was trying to sue her over the broken lease, but since Holly had no actual address, she was never served.

The situation with Joshua had been over a year ago and she hadn't even thought of another man since, she'd been that broken-hearted. She also hadn't lived on her own since then. She brought the three bags containing all her worldly possessions with her when she came with Mr Smith, as the girl whose couch she'd been sleeping on had asked her to take her junk with her on the gig and to find somewhere else to live when it was over.

But now she couldn't help thinking of Tulsa, of the last warm room she'd had, sleeping on Jenny's couch, even though the girl told her not to come back. It had been a good couch, much better than the pine needles and fallen branches she saw around her now.

Holly looked down at her small charge, finally deciding she didn't have a better idea. 'Eli, do you know which way we should go?'

Eli shrugged. 'No,' he said, his lip starting to quiver.

OK, Holly told herself, squaring her shoulders. You're the adult now. Get a grip. 'We're going this way!' she told Eli, pointing toward a friendly-looking pine tree and, taking Eli's hand, off they went.

SEVEN

DALTON

Well, you can't just stand here, Dalton told himself sternly. You gotta do something. Unfortunately, he had no idea what it was that he was supposed to do. Finding his sister would probably be a good idea. But all he really wanted to do was to go home. Back to his mama's house. Back to the bedroom he'd slept in almost every night since he was brought home from the hospital after he was born. Back to the room where his framed baptismal certificate hung on the wall, with the B-52 model airplane he'd put together when he was eight hanging from a string over his desk, his junior high football pennant, signed by the entire team, the football he received as MVP after the last game of his senior year and his bowling trophies from eight years on the Prophesy County Employees' Bowling League. Back to *his* life, not some fantasy life of white picket fences and ladies in twin sweater sets with pearls.

'Mary Ellen!' he yelled into the night. 'I'm leaving! Mary Ellen! You hear me? I'm going home!'

There was no answer, but Dalton hadn't really expected one.

JEAN'S STORY

Angela had agreed to meet me in fifteen minutes at a coffee shop two blocks away from her office building. I drank two cups of coffee while waiting for her, wondering if she'd actually show up. Finally, she did: a tall, thin, lovely young woman in a short wool skirt and matching jacket, her dark brown hair falling straight and slightly beyond her shoulders.

She looked around furtively and then slipped into the seat across from me.

'I really don't know what I'm doing here,' she said.

'And I appreciate you taking this risk,' I said, smiling at her. 'I'm not trying to get Melinda in any trouble – or you, for that matter. This has to do with someone else entirely.'

'Oh.' Angela sounded slightly disappointed. 'Well, whatever.'

'Has she ever mentioned anyone by the name of Emil Hawthorne?' I asked.

'That shrink she was seeing?' Angela asked, her eyes big.

'Yes,' I replied. 'What do you know about him?'

Angela shrugged. 'She saw him for about six months. I made the appointments. Melinda's allergic to dialing a phone, you know.'

I nodded my understanding of an underling's place in the world. 'Did she ever say anything about him?' I asked.

'Not to me,' she said. 'But I heard her on the phone to some girlfriend singing his praises.'

Well, this is getting me nowhere fast, I thought. 'Did she ever see him outside regular office hours?' I asked.

Angela nodded her head. 'Oh, yeah. Sometimes I'd make appointments for late in the afternoon, like six or so, or sometimes at night, like eight o'clock.'

'And you made these appointments through his secretary?' I asked.

Angela shrugged. 'Sometimes. Sometimes I'd talk to the doctor himself.'

Getting excited, I tried to keep my voice calm as I asked, 'When was this . . . that you'd talk to Dr Hawthorne?'

'When I made appointments at night or on the weekend,' she said. Then her eyes got wide. 'Oh!' She began to smile. 'Oh,' she repeated.

MARY ELLEN

To fly or not to fly, Mary Ellen thought, that is the question. She smiled, remembering the English teacher from her senior year and how she loved to quote from *Hamlet*. 'Well, you'd be proud of me now, Mrs Jackson,' Mary Ellen said aloud.

Mary Ellen stood up; the toes of her women's size-twelve Nikes dangling over the edge. She raised her arms like wings and, with a push of her feet, began to fly.

DALTON

Following the reasoning that the minivan was pointed in the direction of a wooded area, where he now found himself, Dalton figured – and hoped – that going the opposite direction would lead him back to the highway.

He was still barefoot, still wearing pants that hit him mid-calf, but he was going home – come hell, high water or sore feet. He headed down the road, trying to keep to the smoother areas where car tires had paved the way and where there was less gravel to hurt his tender feet. It had been a long time since Dalton's feet had been barefoot outdoors, and they were regretting this omission.

It was slow going, but he kept his feet moving and his eyes trained on the horizon, looking for any sign of lights, either the skyline of Tulsa, or just a farmhouse yard light; he didn't care. Any light to show him the way home.

HOLLY

Holly had run away as fast as she could from the barn, considering the fact that she was carrying a four-year-old with breathing problems. But she told herself that this four-year-old was the whole reason to get the hell away from Mr Smith. Of course, he was the whole reason she was in this mess, too, she figured, but she didn't want to dwell on that. 'Can't take this out on a kid,' she told herself. 'It's not his fault. Mostly.'

There was a stand of trees not far from the barn and she'd headed there. She and Eli hunkered down behind a big oak, then watched the barn and waited. There was no sign of Mr Smith. She looked at Eli, who looked back at her, his eyes big.

'Now what?' he whispered.

'Damned if I know,' Holly whispered back.

JEAN'S STORY

'So, you're saying Melinda was screwing the doctor?' Angela said excitedly, leaning on the table, her arms extending so far they almost touched my hands. I pulled back. This woman seemed a little too excited about this entire thing.

'No, of course I'm not saying that,' I said, backpedaling like crazy.

'You are! You are saying that!' Angela said, a gleam in her eye and a smile on her face.

'You really don't like Melinda, do you?' I asked.

'Good God, no! Who would? She's an A-class bitch with a capital "B". The only reason she even has that job is that her uncle owns the company. If she were any good, she'd be a VP or something by now, but she really stinks at what she does. Well, let's face it, Melinda stinks at everything. Except drinking,' Angela said, a smirk on her face. 'She's very, very good at that.'

Angela's lack of compassion – or, more accurately, her lack of humanity – was draining. But she didn't know of the possible abuse Melinda had faced at the hands of Emil Hawthorne.

There must have been something in my expression that gave away my feelings.

Angela's body language spoke volumes. She removed her arms from the table, leaning back. If there hadn't been a back to her chair, she would have landed on the floor.

'It's not my fault Melinda's a bitch!' she said defensively. Then she sighed and moved forward again. 'Look, from day one Melinda treated me like I was dirt, beneath her in too many ways to count. I don't have a college degree, I'm half Hispanic on my mother's side and I can't afford designer fashions. Those are the kinds of things Melinda cares about,' Angela said, a trace of bitterness in her voice.

'I came into this job ready to win friends and influence people, you know, like that old book says? My dad swears by that book. Made all us kids read it.' She shook her head. 'But Melinda . . . How could I win her friendship when she wasn't even in the race?'

'Do you remember how long she saw Dr Hawthorne?' I asked.

'About six months. At first, she was seeing him once every other week. Then once a week. Toward the end, she was seeing him two or three times a week. Then boom. Nothing. Stopped seeing him completely. Just like that.'

I check my notes. 'Around November of last year?' I asked.

She shrugged. 'That sounds right. I know it was before the holidays because she was bitchier than usual around Christmas. Actually kept my Christmas bonus in her desk drawer until after New Year's! Screwed up my Christmas shopping big time. Did it on purpose, too,' Angela said, slumping in her chair as she remembered. 'God, what a bitch.'

PART III
THE SEARCHERS

EIGHT

MILT

'What do you mean?' Clovis Pettigrew asked me. She looked from me to her son-in-law to my wife. 'Are you telling me my grandson's been kidnapped?'

'Yes, Ma'am,' I said, feeling even worse about it now, standing in front of this Mighty Dog of a woman, than I had earlier, if that was at all possible.

'All right, Sheriff. Let's see if I can get this straight,' she said, squaring her shoulders and bringing her body up to its full height of five foot nothing. 'My son's been missing since Thursday night, and, let's let our hair down here, Sheriff: you've got no idea where my boy is. Now you're telling me my four-year-old grandson has been kidnapped. Is this correct?'

'Yes, Ma'am,' I said.

She turned to look at her son-in-law. 'Where's Mary Ellen?'

Hoisting up his two-year-old higher on his hip, Rodney Knight said, 'I wish I knew.'

Clovis Pettigrew turned to me. 'My son, my grandson *and* my daughter?'

I held up my hands in self-defense. 'I got nothing to do with that!'

'She asked me to watch Eli because she had a family emergency,' Jean told Miz Pettigrew. Jean was sitting on the couch, flanked on one side by her business partner, Anne Louise, and on the other by their secretary, DeSandra.

'And you did such a fine job of helping out,' Dalton's mama said sarcastically.

Jean opened her mouth and looked at me, then closed it. Jean's a bit above getting defensive, although Clovis

Pettigrew could bring out the worst in just about anybody. DeSandra, who must have somehow figured out that Miz Pettigrew's comment was less than flattering to Jean, jumped to her feet.

She got out, 'Listen here, you little freak—' before Jean and Anne Louise managed to wrestle her back down to the couch. Anne Louise clamped her hand over DeSandra's mouth, so that all that came out was 'ah ha arrg ah,' which was a little less offensive than what the girl had had in mind.

Shooting a glare at all three women sitting on the couch and crossing her arms over her chest, Miz Pettigrew turned back to me. 'So tell me what you're doing so I can fix it.'

I sighed. To hell with it, I thought. If she can fix it, more power to her. 'We did a search of the area before the ransom call,' I said. 'Now we got Police Chief Smith here with equipment to record and trace any more calls that come in from the kidnapper. And I got an APB out on both Dalton's and Mary Ellen's cars.'

'So basically, y'all are just standing around with your thumbs up your *be*-hinds.' Then Miz Pettigrew nodded her head. 'OK,' she said. 'Sounds adequate.' Turning to her son-in-law, she said, 'Rodney, give me Junior and you go look for your wife.'

Rodney handed over his son and said, 'Where do you suggest I look, Mama Clovis?'

'Well, start back at your house. Then call Clary Swain, see if she's heard from her . . .'

'*Clary Swain?* Mama Clovis, Mary Ellen hasn't talked to her since high school,' Rodney said.

'Humph. Well, who's her best friend now?' she asked.

Rodney just stared at her, then said, 'Well, I dunno. Me?'

Miz Pettigrew hiked the two-year-old up on one skinny hip and said, 'Humph, I doubt it.'

HOLLY

Holly figured their best bet was to get to a road, but the only way this city girl knew how to do that was to get to the driveway leading to the barn and follow that back to the road. The only problem was that the big barn door was open wide and stared directly at the driveway. How could she get the boy to the driveway and down to the road without being seen by Mr Smith?

Looking at the sky, she noted that the moon was doing its crescent-shaped thing, which did light up the ground a little bit, but there were clouds rolling in the sky also, and they covered the moon every once in a while, darkening the world around her. But she guessed she couldn't count on cloud cover for the entire length of the driveway, especially while dragging a four-year-old with breathing problems along with her. She found herself grinning. God, she thought. I sound just like a commando! Under her breath, she said out loud, 'Holly Humphries, Girl Commando! Coming to a theater near you!'

'Huh?' Eli said, looking up at her, his mouth open in an attempt to get as much air into his little lungs as possible.

Holly shook her head. 'Nothing, honey,' she said, tousling his hair.

'We need to go,' Eli whined. 'I want my mommy.'

Holly sighed. 'I know you do, honey.' She scoped out the territory, just like Holly Humphries, Girl Commando would do. The tree line came up close to the driveway. There weren't a lot of trees in front of the barn, but if they darted from one to the other, they could still follow the driveway to the road and have some shelter from the moonlight.

'OK, Eli, hold onto my hand. We're going to move fast from tree to tree but follow the driveway to the road, OK?'

He nodded his head and they began to move. They'd gone no more than five or six steps when bright light engulfed them.

'There you are!' Mr Smith shouted, shining a large flashlight and catching them like deer in headlights, an unfamiliar expression to both city girl Holly and Chicago-bred 'Smith'.

Holly grabbed Eli, looked behind her at the vast nothingness of the dense trees behind the barn and turned in that direction. Run! she thought to herself and took off.

JEAN'S STORY

*My meeting with Melinda Hayes's secretary really didn't
get me very far. I knew in my heart that Emil Hawthorne
had had an affair with Melinda, but unless she admitted it
and pressed charges, my knowledge and two dollars
wouldn't buy me a biscotti. I had one day to do my sleuthing,
and it was already ten a.m. I went to my car and sat in the
driver's seat, picking up the second file.*

*Missy Mason, twenty-two, suffered from severe scoliosis and
wore braces from the hips down and walked with crutches.
There was a little part of me that felt a faint jolt of superi-
ority – my braces were only on my calves. I leaned back
against the headrest, totally disgusted with myself as the thought
truly registered. Then the thought also registered that braces
up to the hips might be too much trouble for Emil Hawthorne.*

*I flipped to the next patient, LeeLee Novotny, who was
legally blind. It took a moment for me to realize that I'd
done the math wrong when I first pulled this patient's file.
I had been looking for women twenty-five and under. LeeLee
Novotny was* considerably *under. LeeLee was now eighteen
years old, but she'd been less than that when she was seen
by Dr Hawthorne. LeeLee Novotny saw him between the
ages of fourteen and sixteen. Two years Emil Hawthorne
could have been abusing her.*

MARY ELLEN

Mary Ellen Pettigrew Knight's depth perception wasn't
particularly good in the daylight; at night, it was downright
non-existent. Her flight off the cliff into nothingness was
actually a little less than the distance from the roof of a
one-story house. She did a belly flop onto a grassy knoll,
knocking the breath out of her, breaking her nose, her right
hand pinkie finger and rendering her unconscious.

DALTON

Dalton's feet hurt. He found a large rock next to the gravel
road he had been following and sat down, lifting one foot

after the other to check them. His right foot was bleeding. The only item of clothing he had on besides his too-short pants and his undershorts was the new shirt he had bought specifically for his date with 'Sarah'. Looking at it in the paltry moonlight, he noticed it was a little the worse for wear: the right shoulder was torn and there were all sorts of stains on the front of it. He grabbed the right sleeve and pulled. Using the good Oxford cloth sleeve, he gingerly dabbed at his bleeding foot. Knowing he had to keep moving, he tied the sleeve around his bleeding foot and tried standing on it. It felt good; so good, in fact, that he tore off the other sleeve and tied it around his left foot.

Then, just for heck of it, he lifted his voice to the heavens and yelled at the top of his lungs, 'Mary Ellen!' He waited for about ten seconds, heard no response and continued on down the road.

HOLLY

'What was that?' Holly said, pulling Eli down with her to hide behind a bush.

'Huh?' Eli asked.

'Did you hear something?' she whispered to the boy.

'Somebody yelling,' Eli said, trying to whisper back.

They'd lost Smith and his flashlight a good five or ten minutes earlier and had been wandering ever since in what Holly hoped was a straight line.

'That's my mommy,' Eli whispered.

Straining her ears for another sound from the woods, she irritably turned to the boy. 'What?'

'Mary Ellen,' Eli said. 'That's my mommy's name.'

'What's Mary Ellen?' Holly asked, her irritability starting to show.

'The yelling,' Eli said, as patiently as a four-year-old could. 'That man was yelling my mommy's name!'

Holly's eyes opened wide and she put her finger to her lips to quiet Eli. Then they both listened.

EMIL

Emil picked up his cell phone and dialed. When the other end was answered, he said, 'You said this was going to be easy. Well, it's not! They're gone and I can't find them and it's not even the right kid, for God's sake!'

He listened for a minute, starting to calm down. 'OK, OK . . . Yes. I understand,' he said. He smiled. 'I love you too.'

MILT

I decided I couldn't stay in the house any longer. So, putting Anthony in charge of 'headquarters', now my house atop Mountain Falls Road, I got in my Jeep and started driving. I wasn't sure where I was going, but anywhere was better than hanging around Clovis Pettigrew. I admit to feeling a bit of shame for leaving my wife there with her, but not enough to stop me.

I called Charlie Smith on my cell phone. 'How's it going?' he said when he answered, having seen my name on the caller ID, I reckoned. You just can't sneak up on a person anymore.

'Same-o, same-o,' I said. 'Except Clovis Pettigrew showed up at my house and sorta took over.'

'That's Dalton's mama, huh?' Charlie said. 'Haven't had the pleasure.'

'*Pleasure*,' I said, tasting the word in my mouth. 'Not a word one would associate with Clovis Pettigrew.'

Charlie laughed. 'I sorta heard that.' Sobering, he said, 'What can I do here to help?'

I shook my head. 'Hell if I know. Come morning, I'm calling in the state police and maybe the FBI.'

'You called in an Amber Alert?' he asked.

'Yes,' I said, probably a little testily. I mean, I'm not a total dullard. Changing the subject because I didn't have much more in the way of news about any of my missing people, I said, 'You know that guy you were telling me about who died cleaning the bathroom for his wife?'

'Yeah, real shame,' Charlie said.

'I got to remembering I had something similar to that

about fifteen years ago over in Bishop,' I told him. 'Lady reported her husband was unconscious, got there and he was dead as a doornail. Seemed he'd mixed Clorox and ammonia while cleaning a small half bath downstairs. No window. That's what this was, right? Bleach and ammonia?'

'Yeah, that's weird. But I guess it happens. Just goes to prove that cleaning is a woman's job,' Charlie said and laughed.

'No shit. But try proving that to your wife.'

'Well, at the moment I got Luanne convinced I'm either too tired or too stupid to do anything more than play with the kids. We'll see how long I can keep that going.'

I shook my head. Lucky bastard. That's the thing about being married to a psychiatrist. She rarely, if ever, buys that B.S.

EMIL

He had to do something, he knew that, but he didn't know what. Chasing that stupid girl and the boy through the woods had proved to be a little more than he could handle. Even that stupid girl had been able to either outrun or outwit him. Something else that could be laid at the feet of Jean MacDonnell. He had been very sharp eight years before. Sharp enough to have outwitted a four-year-old boy and a girl dumb enough to think she could have an acting career in Tulsa, Oklahoma, for God's sake.

He threw his flashlight across the barn, hitting a bale of hay; the lack of breaking glass and cracking plastic did little to appease his current mood. He wanted to kill something, and he couldn't even kill a damn flashlight.

CHARLIE

Charlie checked on the whereabouts of his officers, then sat back down and got to thinking about what Milt said. How could two men *accidentally* kill themselves in *exactly* the same way? He wondered what the statistics were on people killing themselves by mixing ammonia and bleach.

He didn't want to go home, not with this poor little kid

on the loose somewhere, but he really didn't see what he could do to help. Maybe if he went by the sheriff's office, he could find something to do to help out. Or maybe he could get into Milt's records and look up that old accident.

MARY ELLEN

Mary Ellen came to. There were stars above her, a sliver of moon half-hidden by a cloud. Very pretty, she thought, as she lay there staring upward. It took a full few minutes before she began to wonder why she was laying on hard ground and looking up at the sky.

When she looked around, she realized that she was on a small, rocky precipice overlooking a much longer drop in to, as far as Mary Ellen could see in the darkness, a black abyss. Then the sounds of the waterfall penetrated her brain and she realized where she was: somewhere between the cliff and the pool of water at the bottom of the waterfall. Mary Ellen smiled. She was balanced in space, halfway between earth and Heaven.

She tried to push herself up with her right hand and groaned, landing back on the ground. Her right hand wouldn't support her, and the pain caused by leaning on it brought a clarity to Mary Ellen's brain that she hadn't felt in some time. And, with that clarity, she was able to say quite clearly and succinctly, 'Well, shit.'

DALTON

When, for the third time, he passed the tree with the knot-hole that looked like Richard Nixon's profile, Dalton decided that he might be going in circles. He'd been a Boy Scout, almost made it to Eagle Scout, and normally he'd have done fine getting lost in the woods. But that was only if he had on his own pants, the ones with his keys on the key chain with the mini compass. The pants he was wearing certainly didn't have a compass. Checking out the pockets, he found two fuzzy wintergreen Life Savers, a ticket stub to the 'Way off Broadway' production of *Die Hard: The Musical*, and what appeared to be a grocery list, consisting of bread, Boone's Farm apple wine, cheese, Bud Light, aspirin, Ripple and Alka-Seltzer. Dalton wondered if Luther, the former owner of the pants, had a drinking problem.

He was leaning against Richard Nixon's profile when he heard it. A slithering sound. A sneaky sound. Dalton whirled around, reaching for a sidearm that wasn't there.

EMIL

Emil picked up his cell phone and dialed Jean's number. She answered. 'I decided to kill the boy. When I found out he wasn't yours—' he started.

'No, please!' she said on the other end.

'Already done,' Emil said. 'Now I'm coming for *your* son. After that, who knows? Your husband? Who else do you love, Jean MacDonnell? I'll be glad to kill them all!'

MILT

When I got home, all hell had broken loose. Seemed that the kidnapper had called again, but he didn't stay on the line long enough to trace it. Jean was hysterical, sitting on the couch crying and being held by Clovis Pettigrew. Now that's a sight I never thought I'd see. Anne Louise was on the other side of Jean, patting her back and looking ineffectual, a look not common for her. DeSandra was pacing in front of the fireplace and talking to herself.

I'd left Anthony Dobbins in charge, and he was now standing in the doorway to the living room, trying not to watch what was transpiring inside.

'What's going on?' I asked him.

'Ah, we got a call, Sheriff,' answered Anthony.

'The kidnapper?' I asked, surprise evident in my voice. I really had thought that the first call was a prank.

'Yes, Sir.'

'What'd he say?' I asked.

Anthony looked into the living room and didn't say anything.

'Anthony?' I asked again, 'What did the man say?'

My deputy sighed and then looked at me, more at my mouth than at my eyes. I've never known Anthony to not look me in the eye.

'Anthony?' I said again.

'He said he killed the boy, Sheriff,' Anthony said softly.

My gut clenched up bad. I thought I was gonna be sick. Pulling myself together, I asked, 'Where's the body?'

Anthony shook his head. 'He didn't say. He just said . . . Well, Sir, he said he was coming for your boy next. And then you. Seems he's really got it in for your wife, Sir. He said he'd kill anyone she was close to.'

I walked into the living room and pulled Jean out of the clutches of the well-meaning women. She threw her arms around my neck and I held her like I'd never held her before. To Anthony, I said, 'Go get my boy. Bring him down here. Then nobody goes anywhere, understand?'

'Yes, Sir,' Anthony said, then took the stairs two at a time.

JEAN'S STORY

LeeLee Novotny was now eighteen years old and living on campus at the University of Chicago, a campus I knew like the back of my hand, having spent almost ten years roaming its halls and greens.

The registrar had told me what dorm she was in, and her roommate had told me her class schedule. I caught up with LeeLee outside the chemistry building. There was a picture of her in Hawthorne's psych file, and I recognized her immediately. She hadn't changed much in the four years since the picture was taken. She was a small young woman, about five foot, two inches at the most, slight of build, maybe clocking in at 100 pounds or less. She still looked no more than the fourteen years of age she'd been when that picture was taken. Her straight white-blonde hair touched her waist and her watery blue eyes were covered with inch-thick glasses. She was wearing jeans a couple of sizes too large and a T-shirt that could have belonged to an older brother.

The oversized clothes only emphasized her small frame and underage appearance.

I knew from her file that her blindness had been the psychological result of trauma as a young child. She'd seen her mother in bed with another man and, like the rock opera Tommy, she'd been told she'd seen nothing. And, from that day on, she didn't. Dr Hawthorne had brought this out, but by the age of fourteen, the damage to the eye muscles was permanent, and even with extreme exercises she was only able to get back a bit of her sight. Looking at her now, I could only assume that the thick glasses were the positive end result of her time with Dr Hawthorne. But I wondered what else had transpired in that two-year period? Was there a negative end result as well?

'LeeLee?' I said, walking up to her.

She stopped and looked up at me. 'Yes, Ma'am?' she said, in a little squeak of a voice.

'I wonder if you would have a minute to talk with me?' I'd checked her schedule and knew she had an hour between classes.

'What about?' she asked, averting her eyes from mine.

'Emil Hawthorne,' I said.

Her eyes shot up toward mine and then quickly looked away. 'I gotta get to class,' she said, and started walking away.

'LeeLee,' I said, following, 'I know you don't have a class right now.'

'I have to meet somebody,' she said, her short legs moving fast, almost too fast for me on my crutches to keep up with.

'I know what happened with Dr Hawthorne,' I threw out.

The girl immediately stopped in her tracks. Then she burst into tears.

CHARLIE

Milt had gone home by the time Charlie got to the sheriff's office. Gladys was still there, as well as Lonnie Sturgis, both on the phones. Charlie went back to the interrogation room, which also served as Milt's file room. The files were never locked, unless they were holding someone for inter-rogation. One thing about Miss Gladys, Charlie thought, the woman does know how to run a filing system: in chrono-logical *and* alphabetical order. Milt had said the case was from fifteen years back, so Charlie went back eighteen, just to be on the safe side. He had no name, so the alphabet-ical system didn't do him any good. He pulled up a chair from the interrogation table and set to work.

DALTON

Dalton whirled around, toward the sound of whatever it was in the bushes, wishing like hell he had his sidearm, which was currently safe in the locked glove compartment of his car, in a parking lot somewhere in Tulsa.

He crouched by the tree and began to pray.

HOLLY

Holly and Eli snuck through the brush; Holly bent over, Eli holding her hand for dear life. Holly could feel his little body shaking as they approached the clearing from where they'd heard Eli's mother's name called.

Sticking their heads through the brush and into the clearing, they heard a scream. They both screamed back.

NINE

DALTON

Dalton stopped screaming when the apparitions *started* screaming. He stood up and the apparitions stopped screaming as well, before a small voice said, 'Unca Dalton?'

In a daze, Dalton walked forward and Eli burst out from the bushes to fling himself at his uncle. Reflexively, Dalton picked up his nephew in his arms, holding him tight. Behind him, a young woman stood up, a menacing look on her face. 'Who are you? Let go of him!'

'He's my unca Dalton!' Eli shouted and then started to gasp for breath.

Holly rushed toward him and handed him his inhaler.

'Who are you?' Dalton demanded.

'Are you part of the rescue team?' Holly asked.

'What rescue team?' Dalton asked.

'Weren't you looking for us?'

'I don't even know who you are. And what are you doing with my nephew? Where's Mary Ellen?' Dalton demanded. 'Where's Rodney?'

'Who's Rodney?' Holly asked.

Dalton put his nephew's feet back on the ground, his hand resting on the boy's shoulder, holding him close. 'If you ask another question, I'm going to shoot you,' he said. 'Now, *you* answer *my* questions. I'm a duly appointed deputy in Prophesy County and *I* ask the questions!'

'Like hell you do!' Holly said, hands on hips. 'How do I know you're really related to Eli? You could be part of Mr Smith's gang! Eli, come here!'

'Eli, stay!' Dalton said. 'Who's Mr Smith? Never mind that, who are you?'

Eli pulled away from his uncle, planted his feet firmly on the ground and moved his arms like an umpire yelling safe; instead, Eli yelled, 'Stop!'

Both adults looked down at the small boy. Looking at Holly, Eli said, 'He's my unca.' Then, looking at Dalton, he said, 'A mean man took me away from John's house.' Eli pointed at Holly. 'She took me away from the mean man.' Glancing from one to the other, he summed up with, '"Kay?'

Both adults nodded. Then Dalton said, 'Who was the mean man?'

'Mr Smith,' Holly and Eli said in unison. Holly pulled Eli close to her. 'I'm not really sure *who* he is,' she admitted to Dalton, lowering her head. 'He hired me in Tulsa to do an acting gig – he *said*.' She made a ladylike snort. 'Some acting gig!'

'You're an actress?' Dalton asked.

Holly lifted up her head proudly. 'Yes, I am. But Mr Smith certainly is *not* a director.'

Dalton stared at Holly for a moment, then asked, 'Are you just acting here, or are you really a woman?'

MILT

All three kids, Johnny Mac and Dalton's eleven-year-old niece Rebecca and two-year-old nephew Rodney, Jr were planted in front of the TV in the living room, a cartoon movie playing with the sound down low. Clovis Pettigrew had taken up the pacing in front of the fireplace and DeSandra was sitting in an easy chair facing the couch, where I sat holding my wife, with Anne Louise on Jean's other side.

'What can I do to help?' DeSandra asked, leaning forward.

I shook my head. I had no idea what anyone could do. No idea what *I* could do, and I was the one who should be having the ideas.

'I know!' DeSandra said, brightening visibly. 'Pizza!'

Her two employers ignored her while I stared at her like she was the idiot I believed her to be. Then I looked at the kids in front of the TV. It was going to be a long night.

'Yeah,' I said to DeSandra. 'That's a good idea. Why don't you order some pizza? But make sure Anthony answers the door when the delivery man gets here, OK?'

'Why? Oh!' DeSandra said and pointed a finger at my nose. 'Got'ja!'

And with that, she headed for the phone.

JEAN'S STORY

We ended up in LeeLee's dorm room. The roommate I'd spoken to earlier was absent, presumably in class. The room-mate's side of the dorm room was covered with snapshots and pictures pulled from magazines, a brightly colored Indian bedspread covering the bed and semi-dead roses in a vase on her half of the metal partners' desk that divided the room. T-shirts and tops littered the bed, and jeans and underpants all but covered her half of the floor.

LeeLee's side of the room was immaculately clean, as I'm sure is necessary for any person with a sight challenge, but it was also barren. No pictures on the walls, nothing but braille and large-print books on the desk; a white blanket the only cover on the bed.

It was as if LeeLee had been waiting for someone to want to know her secret, because I didn't even have to ask – she was that ready to tell what had happened to her.

I wasn't that aware of it then, but the story LeeLee told me is entirely too common in the healing professions – actually, in any profession where a person with a certain personality flaw is put in a position of authority over another person. Dentists, teachers, doctors, shrinks – you name it. A flawed human being finds a person like LeeLee, young, vulnerable, damaged, and takes advantage in the worst way possible.

However, LeeLee's break with Dr Hawthorne had nothing to do with the fact that he was having sex with her at almost every session. The break came when LeeLee's mother discovered that her daughter's hysterical blindness was caused by her own infidelity. The mother stopped the sessions immediately and forbade LeeLee ever to talk of the sessions again.

So, for the second time, LeeLee was forced to keep another deep, dark secret. Sadly, the damage done to this young woman had been excessive, by both her mother and her therapist. We worked together for a year, along with the DA and the investigator from the American Medical Association, to shut down Emil Hawthorne, but LeeLee never responded to any kind of therapy I tried with her. She was as shut down as we hoped Emil Hawthorne to be.

We had our triumph in the end, but it cost us. Emil Hawthorne was stripped of his license and sentenced to four years in prison and a hefty fine. However, I lost my internship and it took a year to start over at a new hospital. But, worst of all, LeeLee Novotny's mother ended up putting her in a private mental institution that still treated patients with electroshock therapy.

Hawthorne never saw a day of jail, of course. He ended up in a coma from a car accident on the eve of his incarceration. Somehow, that just seemed par for the course for Emil Hawthorne.

MILT

When Jean finished telling me her story, I held her close. 'It's not your fault, babe. None of this is your fault.'

'That's right,' Anne Louise said. 'I remember all this. He was scum, Jean. We both know that. You did the right thing at the time. And besides, he's in a coma. This can't be him. No matter what people want to believe, patients as damaged as Emil just don't come out of comas.'

Jean turned to Anne Louise. 'Call, please,' she begged her. 'Call the hospital in Chicago. See if he's still there.'

Anne Louise sighed but nodded her head and took a cell phone out of her purse.

MARY ELLEN

'Help!' Mary Ellen called. There was no answer. She sat on her little piece of earth, looking up at the stars in the sky, then down to the black pool below. She'd tried to stand up at one point, but her left ankle didn't want to cooperate. So occasionally, she'd sit up and yell 'Help!' to no avail and then lay back down and contemplate her life as it had become.

HOLLY

Holly wasn't sure she trusted this big lummox of a man, but she didn't feel that she had any choice. He said he was a sheriff's deputy, but did that really mean anything? Some hick county sheriff of some hick county she'd never heard of? She'd seen movies about small-town sheriffs and what they did to people – especially good-looking young women like her. *Road Gang Babes* had been one of her ex-boyfriend's favorite videos. But she was just so damn tired.

She looked at her watch, realizing it was already one o'clock in the morning. He said he was Eli's uncle, Eli said he was his uncle. If she couldn't trust Eli, who could she trust? Holly sat down on a fallen log, pulling Eli onto her lap.

'OK, fine,' she said, looking up at the big lummox, who was actually kind of cute when you really looked at him. 'I can't walk another step, Deputy. Can we just sit down for a while?'

Dalton sat down beside her. 'Yeah, that sounds like a really good idea.'

CHARLIE

Charlie had no idea that Milt had had this many cases over the years, but it beat the police department files by a mile. Everything from murder to the great canned-peach caper of 1992, when little old ladies stole canned peaches. Charlie couldn't help reading that file. Who would be able to resist? Six former members of the Longbranch Volunteer Fire Department's Ladies Auxiliary trying to beat out the new, younger members by selling more baked goods at the annual Ladies Auxiliary bake sale. They stole the peaches over a five-month period, hitting six different stores in the county before they were caught. And the women were only caught because Milt was able to tackle one old lady who tried to run away using her walker.

Charlie started laughing. It was late and both his body and his mind were tired, and he just kept laughing until tears streamed down his face.

MILT

It had taken a while at this time of night for Anne Louise to get through to the Chicago rehab center where Emil Hawthorne had been in a coma for the past eight years. But once she got through to someone on the right floor, the information was instantaneous. Anne Louise put it on speakerphone so we could all hear.

'Oh, yes,' the floor nurse said when Anne Louise asked

about Hawthorne. 'A real success story! Dr Hawthorne just woke right up – maybe a little over eight months ago! You coulda knocked us all over with just one feather!' the nurse said, and laughed. 'And the strangest thing, he had almost complete recall. Of his accident and everything. And in less than two months he was up and walking and talking, feeding himself. It was a real miracle!'

'Do you know where he is now?' Anne Louise asked.

'No. Maybe outpatient PT knows. He should be seeing them on a weekly basis, but I really don't know about that. And they're closed now. But they'll open at eight in the morning.'

'Thank you so much,' Anne Louise said and hung up.

She and Jean just looked at each other. I rubbed Jean's neck. 'So? What does this mean?' I asked

'It means Emil Hawthorne is out there somewhere and he's killed Eli and he's after John!' Jean answered.

Anne Louise grabbed Jean's hands and held them tight. 'We don't know that, Jean,' she said. 'If it is Emil, he wouldn't . . . he couldn't . . .'

'Kill Eli?' Jean said softly, hoping the boy's family couldn't hear her. 'You know what he was capable of before the coma, Anne Louise. Waking up with total recall? That's unheard of. But if he did, and with that much anger all directed at me, we have no idea what he's capable of now!'

I called Charlie Smith on his cell phone and asked for an APB to be put out on Emil Hawthorne, giving him what little details I had.

'You think this is the guy?' he asked.

'Jean thinks so. He's our only suspect at this point,' I said.

'Well, we'll find the bastard, Milt. Don't worry about that,' Charlie said.

'From your mouth to God's ear,' I said, remembering my mama's favorite saying, and hung up.

It was after one o'clock in the morning when Rodney Knight came back to the house.

'I can't find her,' he said to his mother-in-law, then burped.

Standing, hands on hips, Clovis Pettigrew said, 'You mean she wasn't at the Dew Drop Inn?'

'Ah—' Rodney started, and then he just stopped, as he had nothing left to say.

'Well, while you were out drinking, the kidnapper called!' Clovis started, getting close to her son-in-law and staring up into his face.

Jean stood up. 'Stop it, Clovis. The kids.'

Clovis sighed and moved away from Rodney. 'Get your children in my car and I'll drive y'all home,' she said. When Rodney failed to move, Clovis shouted, 'Now!' Rodney moved.

'Miz O'Donnell, Chief,' DeSandra said, 'I gotta be heading home, too. Thanks, I had a nice time.' I couldn't help staring at her. How could one person get so much wrong in a single sentence?

Anne Louise kissed Jean on the cheek and hugged me. 'I need to get home, too,' she said. 'If there's anything . . .'

Jean hugged her. 'I'll call you if there is.'

Anne Louise nodded and headed out the door behind DeSandra and Clovis Pettigrew and what appeared to be left of her family.

That just left me and Jean and Johnny Mac. And Anthony Dobbins.

'Sheriff,' Anthony said. 'I'm staying. I'll be right here in the living room drinking coffee if you need me.'

I nodded as I led my family to the master bedroom. Johnny Mac wasn't getting out of my reach tonight. 'Thanks, Anthony,' I said. 'Help yourself to the pizza or anything in the fridge.'

''Night, Sheriff. Dr MacDonnell.'

EMIL

Emil watched the car come up the long driveway. He moved toward it, tired, irritated and totally out of sorts.

When the electric window rolled down, he said, 'Well, it's about damn time you got here.' The words had barely left his mouth when the automatic appeared in the driver's gloved hand, and one shot was fired between Emil Hawthorne's charismatic dark blue eyes.

MARY ELLEN

As the sun rose on Sunday morning, it cleared the mountain top where Falls Creek crested and dropped 100 feet into the pool below, finally slowing as it became once again Falls Creek, flowing onward downstream. The flow of the upper section of Falls Creek had slowed, causing the waterfall to now trickle lazily down into the pool.

As the sun came over the mountain top, over the small precipice on which Mary Ellen lay, it shone directly onto her closed eyelids, forcing them to blink and Mary Ellen to awaken. Shielding her eyes with a hand, she sat up and looked down into the former abyss. It was no longer there. Instead, maybe half a story below lay the pool at the end of the waterfall, shining bright green in the sunlight, with Falls Creek flowing from it. Wild flowers dotted the meadow, and a pregnant doe fed on the tall grasses. Mary Ellen decided that she'd died during the night and was now watching Heaven, wondering how soon she would be admitted.

DALTON

Dalton woke up with a crick in his neck. His nephew Eli was curled spoon-style against his belly, and that crazy actress girl was curled spoon-style against his back. He seemed to be the middle spoon, and he was afraid to move, lest he wake up one or the other. He had no real qualms about waking Eli – his little nephew had awakened him many an early morning when staying over at Grandma Clovis's house. But he felt a little strange waking up the girl. This was the first time he'd ever spent the night with a woman, really, even though it wasn't . . . well, you know. But still, he was a little embarrassed. About that and about the . . . well, the *tightness*, for want of a better word, around the front of his pants. That happened a lot in the mornings when he first woke up, but it seemed to be even a little tighter, and getting tighter still as he felt the warmth from the female body spooned up against his back. He scooted a little closer to Eli, away from Holly, but she just scooted right up next to him again. There was no escaping either laying there with tight pants or waking up both of them.

Thinking fast – well, as fast as Dalton *could* think – he jumped up from his position in the middle of the spoon rack, said, 'Gotta go pee,' and took off for the privacy of the woods.

CLOVIS PETTIGREW

Clovis sat in her favorite chair, a straight-backed armchair positioned on the outskirts of her living room, her toes planted firmly on the floor (the only part of her feet that could reach the ground), and made her decision. She stood up and walked to the wall phone in the kitchen and dialed the number she'd looked up in the middle of the night.

When the ringing stopped, a recorded voice said, 'This is the Oklahoma City office of the Federal Bureau of Investigation . . .'

MILT

The phone woke me up at eight thirty in the morning. I croaked out, 'Hello?'

'Sheriff Kovak?' a female voice said.

'Yeah?' I managed.

'This is Lee Anne Carmody, Agent Carmody, with the FBI? We worked together on that bank robbery—'

'Yeah, Agent Carmody.' Scully. The redhead with the partner who looked like Mulder. Who could forget 'em? 'What?'

'I got a call from a lady in your town, name of Clovis Pettigrew.'

'Ah, shit,' I said.

'She says her son, her daughter and her grandson have all been kidnapped and there's been a ransom demand on the grandson. Any of this true?'

'We got a ransom demand,' I said, taking the phone and moving into the kitchen so that Johnny Mac wouldn't wake up and hear any of this, 'but then got another call saying the victim had been killed. We haven't found a body yet, so I can't tell you anything more than that. As for her son, Dalton, you met him. He's one of my deputies, the big guy . . .'

'Oh, yeah, the cute one.'

Cute? I thought. Different strokes. 'Yeah, well he's been missing for a few days, but I think he's just off with a lady friend. But as for his sister, the mother of the missing boy – man, I just don't know. She told my wife she had a family emergency and took off. Left her boy with us . . .'

'With you?' Agent Carmody asked, her voice a little less friendly.

'Yeah, with me,' I said, letting my irritation show. 'The boy was with me when he was abducted. It's my fault. All my fault. Now, can we move on?'

'I didn't say a word, Sheriff,' Agent Carmody said.

'Look, let me check in with my people and see what's going on. I'll call you back if we need assistance. That all right with you, Agent Carmody?'

'I'll wait for your call, Sheriff,' she said, and rang off.

MARY ELLEN

Mary Ellen watched the Heavenly world beneath her, marveling at God's wisdom in making Heaven so perfect in every way. She watched as a baby bunny rabbit came out of its hole and looked around, and, even from her high perch, Mary Ellen could see its tiny nose twitch as it sniffed the air. What she didn't see until it was all but over was the large hawk swoop down and grab the baby bunny in its talons, rising again to the sky as it took its prey home for an early supper.

That's when Mary Ellen realized that she probably wasn't watching Heaven after all. She looked up at the cliff above her, realizing it wasn't exactly a cliff. More of a steep hill. She grabbed onto a root sticking out of the hill and pulled herself to her feet. Her ankle seemed stronger this morning. She found a toehold on the hillside and stepped up, finding more steps and more roots and small trees to help pull herself up the hill, until she reached the top.

She stood there looking around, trying to get her bearings. She was still in the woods. She couldn't remember exactly where she'd left the car. Oops. And Dalton. She'd forgotten about Dalton. She hoped he was OK, but then thought, 'He's a big boy; he can take care of himself.' She was tired of being the one to take care of everybody else. Her little brother could surely fend for himself. Now that she'd gotten him out of jail, anyway.

Then she heard a small voice, a little loud and a little on the whiny side, say, 'But I'm hungry!'

She followed the sound until she came to a small clearing. In the middle of the clearing was a fallen log. Sitting on that log was a young woman Mary Ellen had never seen before. On her lap sat Mary Ellen's son, Eli, and standing in front of them both was Mary Ellen's younger brother Dalton.

'Hi,' Mary Ellen said. 'What's going on?'

EMIL

Emil Hawthorne lay on the ground where his killer had left him. The life had drained out of him rather quickly and there was really nothing left of him now but food for scavengers – the birds and mice and bugs that fed off human remains. His drama was over; no more revenge for the lost years, no more hatred, or envy, jealousy or even love – not that there had ever been much of that. No, Emil Hawthorne lay on the ground, very little blood flowing from the wound between his eyes. Death had been almost instantaneous; it had stopped the heart from beating and thus the blood from pumping. Without the smell of blood, some of the predators would take a little longer to get there; others had their own timetables. But really, none of that mattered to Emil Hawthorne anymore.

MILT

Anthony Dobbins was asleep on the living-room couch. A half-eaten slice of cheese pizza lay on his stomach, an open can of Dr Pepper sat on the coffee table. One leg was on the floor, the other on the couch, the one hand on his chest was the hand caressing the pizza and the other arm slung over his head, with its hand resting in his short-cropped black hair. His mouth was open and the sounds coming out of it were not exactly snores – more like little snorts and wheezes. I couldn't help wondering how Anthony's wife dealt with it.

'Anthony,' I said, shaking the arm slung over his head.

He snorted, his eyes popped open and he sat up quickly and said, loudly, 'I'm awake!'

'Good,' I said. 'We got a call from the FBI. We need to check in with our people. See what's going on. If we don't find something pretty soon, we're gonna have the Feebies up our collective asses.'

'I'm awake!' Anthony said again, blinking rapidly.

HOLLY

Holly stood up, with Eli squirming in her arms. 'Mama!' the boy shouted and Holly set him down. He ran to his mother, who knelt down and hugged him.

'Geez, Mary Ellen!' Dalton rushed up to his sister. 'Where have you been?' Looking at her bruised and battered person, he asked, 'Are you OK?'

Holly stood back, a little shy about the family reunion. She had never been involved in anything like that, having been raised in various foster homes.

But then Eli grabbed his mother's hand and dragged her toward Holly. 'Mama, this is my friend Holly. She saved me.'

Holly held out her hand to Mary Ellen, but Eli's mother just looked at Holly's hand, a confused look on her face. By the time Mary Ellen raised her hand to shake Holly's, Holly had already lowered hers. Holly raised hers again, but Mary Ellen had lowered hers. Then they looked at each other and laughed awkwardly.

'Well, thank you,' Mary Ellen said. 'For saving Eli.' She frowned. 'Exactly how did that come about?' she asked.

Everyone started to talk at once, just as the black clouds closed in and the heavens opened up with a heavy downpour of rain. Lightning struck the tallest tree near the clearing and everyone stopped talking – in order to scream.

MILT

My second-in-command, Emmett Hopkins, called in at 9:05.
'Milt, we found Mary Ellen Knight's car,' he said.
'And Mary Ellen?' I asked.
'Not so much. Door's open, key's in the ignition, battery's dead as a doornail. She mighta gone looking for a phone or something. Car's over here by the falls, maybe two miles from your house. You know how bad cell reception is out here.'
'Any signs of foul play?' I asked.
'Well, looks like some dried blood, but it's in the passenger seat,' Emmett said.
In stereo, from the phone in my hand and from outside my house, I heard the sound of thunder and through the window saw the deluge of rain that had just begun. Springtime in Oklahoma.
'Shit!' Emmett said. 'Gotta go!'
'Keep me posted!' I shouted back, not sure that Emmett had heard me, but I knew that he would do it anyway. I stared out the window as the heavens erupted, the rain falling so hard that water was rushing in streams through my driveway and yard already. I wondered about little Eli, if he was still alive and caught in this, or if his little body was being washed farther away, so far that we might never find it.

HOLLY

As the tree struck by lightning began to splinter, large limbs began to fall. Dalton grabbed Eli, his sister and Holly, wrapping his arms around all three and pushing them to the ground, using his large body to try to shield them. A limb hit Dalton in the back, its branch catching him on the head.

He passed out. It took both Mary Ellen and Holly to get Dalton's unconscious body off Eli.

Eli, who some might say had had just about enough, was crying hysterically. Seeing that his mother was not responding, Holly picked him up in her arms and found an overhanging rock to sit under, leaving Dalton and his sister behind. The lightning rent the sky, the thunder exploded around them, and the rain was coming down so hard that Holly and her small charge were actually sitting in a puddle. They shivered and held each other tight, both knowing that their nightmare wasn't over yet.

MARY ELLEN

Mary Ellen was confused. It was a state she was getting used to. She was very wet, her brother was lying dead or unconscious in front of her and the girl, Holly, had taken her son and run off. She wasn't sure what she was supposed to do at this point. She figured her son should probably be her priority, but then she thought he might actually be better off with the girl. Then she thought that perhaps she should try to help Dalton, see if he was still alive. But her overwhelming concern at the moment, the thing she really wanted to take care of, was the wet. She just didn't want to be wet anymore.

Dalton moaned and Mary Ellen decided that he probably wasn't dead. She tapped him on the shoulder. 'Dalton?' she shouted over the roar of the rain.

Dalton rolled onto his side, wiping mud from his eyes. 'Mary Ellen?' he shouted back.

'It's raining!' Mary Ellen yelled.

Dalton nodded his head. 'Help me stand up?' he asked. Mary Ellen stood and held out her hand, helping Dalton to his feet. 'Where are Eli and that girl?' Dalton yelled.

Mary Ellen shrugged her shoulders. 'They took off after the tree hit you!' she shouted over the pounding rain.

As abruptly as the rain started, it stopped – at least to a drizzle – the absence of the sound of pounding rain a miracle in and of itself. From the trees came Holly, carrying Eli.

'You two OK?' Dalton asked.

Holly nodded. 'I thought you were dead.'

Dalton grinned his big, lopsided grin. 'Kinda hard to kill me,' he said.

Holly smiled back. 'Good, because I don't know where the heck we are and I'm afraid your sister's not much use.'

Dalton looked at Mary Ellen, who was smiling kindly at one and all.

'Maybe you're right,' he said. 'Mary Ellen?'

His sister turned to him. 'Yes?'

'You OK?' Dalton asked.

She shrugged. 'What does that really mean?'

Dalton shrugged back and picked up his nephew in his arms. 'Let's get out of here,' he said, leading the way.

EMMETT HOPKINS

Hearing a commotion from the woods, Emmett looked up to see a band of disreputable-looking people heading towards him. He noticed Dalton Pettigrew leading the pack. Looking at his junior deputy, Emmett asked, 'Where are your shoes, boy? And your pants?'

Dalton grinned. 'Long story,' he said.

MILT

I got a second call from Emmett about twenty minutes after the rain stopped.

'Milt, you sitting down?' he asked.

I thought, Oh shit, and sat down on my living-room couch. 'Give it to me,' I said.

'Dalton just walked up to his sister's car, with his sister, his nephew and a pretty young lady I don't know in tow. Looks like all's well, Milt.'

And, for maybe the second – OK third – time in my adult life, I cried.

PART IV
WHODUNNIT?

TEN

MILT

I made two calls first thing; the first was to Special Agent Lee Anne Carmody, telling her all was well; the second was to the physical therapy department of the rehab center where Emil Hawthorne had been in a coma for eight years. I needed to know if he was still around and still getting his physical therapy like he should be.

The call to Agent Carmody went about as I'd expected it would.

'So, you fucked up but it turned out OK. That about it?' Agent Carmody asked.

'Yep, that's about it,' I answered.

She laughed. 'I swear to God, Kovak, you've got the luck of the Irish like nobody I've ever seen.'

'And mostly I'm Polish, on my father's side. I think.'

'Go figure,' she said and hung up.

The call to the rehab hospital in Chicago took a little bit longer. In fact, I had to finally get Jean to do it since she'd been on the staff at the hospital that ran the rehab center and her being a doctor seemed to carry more weight than me being a county sheriff in Oklahoma. As Agent Carmody would and did say, go figure.

The gist of it was that Emil Hawthorne's physical therapist, a guy named Burt Sanchez, hadn't seen Dr Hawthorne in over six weeks.

'He just stopped coming,' Sanchez told Jean. 'I called the halfway house where he was staying and they said he moved out. That's the last I heard of him.'

I decided that I needed Jean with me during the interview with the girl who'd been hired by Hawthorne, the one who showed up with Dalton and Eli. So I sent Anthony home to get some sleep, and we packed up Johnny Mac

and headed to Bishop to drop him off at my sister's house.
Then Jean and me headed for the sheriff's department.

HOLLY

It wasn't what she had expected. She'd had visions of a street
in an old Western movie, a horse tied up to a hitching post
in front of a door with a sheriff's star painted on it. Instead,
Dalton drove Mary Ellen's newly charged-up minivan to an
ugly cinder block building painted an even uglier brown. White
letters spelled out PROPHESY COUNTY LAW CENTER on the outside
of the building. Inside was scarred linoleum flooring with
orange plastic chairs up against the walls, and a waist-high
plywood partition, painted the same ugly brown as the outside
of the building – like it would cost more to get a different
color – covered in mustard-colored Formica and cutting the
room in half. A stern-looking woman stood at the very center
of the partition, arms folded across her chest.

'Dalton Pettigrew, you are in very deep doo-doo,' the
stern-looking woman said. Then her eyes flooded with tears
as she opened a hidden flap in the Formica top and came
out, throwing her arms around Dalton and Mary Ellen, then
kneeling to hug Eli.

Holly stood back at this, yet another family reunion. These
people sure seem to love each other, she thought. That's
when the front door opened and a woman barely taller than
Eli came rushing in, followed by a very tall man and two
more children. This, she finally figured out, was Mary
Ellen's family, including Mary Ellen and Dalton's mother,
the very little woman who seemed to be in charge.

With all the shouting and crying and carrying on, the
deputy who had rescued them, Emmett Hopkins, came out
of a back room. 'Y'all simmer down, now. We've got to
interview everybody separate, OK? Don't y'all go telling
your stories now to just anybody—'

'And who, pray tell, are you calling "just anybody",
Emmett Hopkins?' the little woman asked.

'Miz Pettigrew, we gotta wait for the sheriff to get
here—' Deputy Hopkins started.

'And why isn't he here now?' Miz Pettigrew demanded. 'You'd think that, in a situation like this, he'd be front and center, not off gallivanting around town . . .'

'He's taking his son to his sister's . . .'

'Now, why would I care about that?' the little woman demanded.

Holly walked over to one of the orange plastic chairs and sat down. Eli came up to her and crawled in her lap. The crow-like voice of Eli's grandmother lulled them both to sleep.

MILT

Everybody was talking at once when I walked in the front door of the sheriff's department. Everybody, that is, except Eli and the young woman who'd been with Hawthorne, both of whom appeared to be asleep, sitting in a chair in the front room.

'OK, y'all,' I said loudly, 'and that means you, Miz Pettigrew, everybody just shut up!'

Which they all did since I was being so rude. Instead, they all turned to stare at me. I musta woke up Eli, because he began to whimper. His mama went over to him and picked him up outta the girl's arms. The girl stood up, moving closer to Dalton, I noticed.

'First off,' I said, 'I need y'all separated. Dalton, take your sister into Emmett's office and close the door. Her in there, you in my office. Close that door and you stay there.'

I waited while Dalton digested this information and then moved off down the hall to do as I'd told him. Then I said, 'Miss Gladys, if you'd be so kind as to take Mr Eli here back to the break room and buy him a cup of cocoa, I'd be much obliged.'

Gladys may shoot daggers at me on an hourly basis, but when it comes to kids, she's a grandma and can't seem to get over that. She smiled at Eli and he went with her willingly.

'Miz Pettigrew, Rodney,' I said to Mary Ellen's mama and husband, 'you and the little ones stay out here or go

home, that's your prerogative. Now, Miss Humphries, is
it?' I asked, turning to the girl who'd been with Hawthorne.
   She nodded her head.
   'I'd like you to come with me to the interrogation room.'
I smiled when she blanched at the word. 'Not as bad as it
sounds,' I said. 'My wife here is gonna come with us.'
   The girl smiled tentatively at Jean and Jean smiled back.
'Jean, you wanna take her on back?' I said, and watched
while the two women left.
   Turning to the remaining bunch, I said, 'Miz Pettigrew,
you staying?'
   'You bet your ass,' she said, and sat her ass down firmly
in one of our orange visitor chairs.
   I shrugged and headed back to the interrogation room.

CHARLIE

Charlie was fast asleep, his head, right arm and half his
chest draped over the open file cabinet for 1995. When Jean
MacDonnell and Holly Humphries came in the room, he
woke up, raising his head to look at them, a string of drool
hanging between his bottom lip and the file on Mac Durby,
arrested for indecent exposure on April 12, 1995.
   'Charlie?' Jean said.
   'Huh?' Charlie said.
   Milt came in the room. 'Charlie, what the hell?'
   'Milt,' Charlie said. He looked at Jean. 'Hey, Jean.'
   'Hey, Charlie,' she said.
   'What are you doing, man?' Milt asked.
   'Oh,' he said, rubbing at the string of drool and then at
his sleep-encrusted eyes. 'Ah, I was looking through your
files . . .'
   'I see that!' Milt said, a little testily.
   Charlie stood up, rubbing his back and stretching out his
legs. 'It's about that case of mine—' Charlie started.
   'Charlie, can't you see I got bigger fish to fry here? You
know, a kidnapping and all?' Milt said.
   Charlie nodded his head. 'I suppose so. I'll just get out
of your way,' he said, and started for the door.

Milt put up a hand to stop him. 'Just hold on, Charlie.' Turning to his wife and Holly Humphries, Milt said, 'Ladies, could y'all excuse us a minute? Just wait in the hall for just a minute.'

Jean raised an eyebrow but escorted Holly out of the room.

'Now what?' Milt asked.

'I just got to wondering about the case you had that was similar to this one,' Charlie said.

'What one?' Milt said, the exasperation obvious in his voice.

'The ammonia/bleach one!' Charlie said, a little irritated himself after having spent the night sleeping on a file drawer.

'Oh, that. What about it?' Milt asked.

'Just want to see the file on it, that's all.'

'Humph,' Milt said. He shut the file drawer for 1995 and opened the one for 1997. 'Think it was here,' he said. He rifled through until he found it. 'Albert Canfield. One domestic disturbance in eighty-five, then OD'd on ammonia and bleach in ninety-seven. Left a widow and a teenaged daughter.'

'Can I see that?' Charlie asked, taking the file from Milt's hand as he asked. The widow's name was Roberta Canfield, and the teenaged daughter, fourteen at the time, was named Carolina. Hell of a coincidence, Charlie thought.

DALTON

Dalton had never been alone in Milt's office before. The door was closed and nobody could see him, so he looked around a little. Right on the desk was the wedding picture of him and Dr Jean, in a double frame with a picture of him and Dr Jean bringing Johnny Mac home from the hospital. Dalton felt sad looking at that picture. He'd thought for a little while that that was gonna be his life, too. Him and Sarah. Except there was no Sarah. Only some guy named Geoffrey who thought it was fun to dress up in women's clothes.

Memories were coming back. Bits and pieces that Dalton

was trying to put in some chronological order. He remembered, even in his earlier drunkenness, the truth he'd learned. That Sarah wasn't Sarah, but Geoffrey. Some guy dressed in women's clothes. He remembered that big, oversized purse Sarah – no, Geoffrey – carried. When Sarah was with Dalton, Geoffrey had been in that bag, and when Geoffrey showed up, Sarah had been put back in that bag, never to come out for Dalton again.

Tears welled in his eyes as he remembered the pain he felt, realizing Sarah had never been. He wanted to hit the man, that Geoffrey, but it seemed that Geoffrey hadn't really meant to hurt him; he had thought Dalton knew. And anyway, if you looked at it in a certain light, hitting Geoffrey would be the same as hitting Sarah.

He'd run out of the bar where they'd been drinking mojitos, run into the night, slobbering drunk, crying, no better than the people he put in jail on a Saturday night to sober up for church on Sunday.

He remembered quieting down some and trying to find his car. But he had no idea where he was or where his car was, either. And then he met those boys. One had his hat on backwards and one had on a lot of jewelry. The third one's pants were too big and almost falling off him. Or had it all been one guy? Dalton wasn't sure. All he knew was that one minute he was standing there telling those guys that the watch on his arm was all that he had left of his daddy, and the next minute he woke up pantsless in an alley.

Dalton shook his head at the folly of his entire weekend.

He wondered if he was gonna spend the rest of his life in the same bedroom of his mama's house where he'd always slept. Eat the same food his mama prepared for him every night – meatloaf on Monday, fried chicken on Tuesday, sausage on Wednesday, Salisbury steak on Thursday and Hamburger Helper on Friday. Saturday was sandwiches and Sunday was dinner at the cafeteria after church. Then going to work every morning with a brown bag loaded with a chopped ham sandwich, a bag of chips, an apple, orange or banana, depending on the day. Coming home every night to watch 'Jeopardy' with his mama, eat his dinner and go to bed. Was that gonna be his life forever?

He thought about the girl now being interviewed by Milt. She was pretty, yeah, but she was an actress. Way too sophisticated for him. A city girl, like Sarah, but real, where Sarah hadn't been. He liked the way her reddish-brown hair glowed warm under the lights, and the way her brown eyes sparkled when she talked to Eli. She was real good with Eli, which meant she'd probably be a real good mother . . .

Stop it! Dalton told himself sternly. Just stop it! Hadn't he made a big enough fool of himself already this weekend? Thinking like that about a girl like Holly Humphries, a real-live actress who'd probably be off to Hollywood in a New York minute she was that good.

Dalton sighed and opened the sheriff's lap drawer to see what was in there.

MILT

I got rid of Charlie Smith, letting him borrow the file he was so hot about, and brought my wife and Holly Humphries back into the interrogation room.

The girl was scared, I could see that right off the bat, so I tried to put her at ease. 'Miz Humphries,' I said, 'if you could give me an address and phone number for you in Tulsa, please.'

'Well, all I have is my cell phone, but that man, Smith, he took that. I don't exactly have an address . . . I've been sorta staying with friends, here and there . . .' Her voice faded out.

Jean caught my eye and it didn't take a rocket scientist to figure out she was telling me to go nice.

'How did you and "Smith" find each other?' I asked her.

'He put an ad on "Craig's List",' Holly said. 'That was before I hocked my laptop and I answered it.' Tears welled up in her eyes. 'I was gonna get my laptop back just as soon as Mr Smith paid me, but now I guess I won't.' Her face crunched up and she began to cry. Which is something I just don't deal with if I can help it. 'I had everything on my laptop!' she wailed. 'My journal and my Facebook and my MySpace and all my music and the addies of all my friends all over the world!' She crumbled at this point and Jean, who was sitting next to her, put an arm around her. Holly wrapped herself around Jean and bawled outright.

I left the room.

Only to be immediately accosted by Hawke Pettigrew, the titular man of the house for the Pettigrew clan, Miz Clovis's oldest child, Mary Ellen's and Dalton's older brother.

He stood just outside the interrogation room door, and I wasn't sure if he'd been listening or not. I didn't know Hawke very well, and wasn't sure if he was the kind to eavesdrop or not. If he was like his mama, yeah. If he was like his little brother, not so much.

'Sheriff,' he said, sticking out his hand for me to shake.

I shook it. 'Hawke, what can I do for you?'

'Just wanted to thank you for taking care of my family,' he said, a shy smile on his face. 'I was at a loss for what to do.'

'Well, it's my job, Hawke.'

'You know, Dalton worships you,' he said out of nowhere.

I felt my face turning hot. 'He's a good man,' I managed to say.

'He found his niche with you, all right,' Hawke said smiling. 'We – Mama and me – were worried he'd never find his place in this world.'

'He's an integral part of our system now,' I told Hawke, not even sure what I meant by that, but feeling like it sounded good.

'Can I take Mama home now?' Hawke asked.

I shook my head. 'Not up to me, Hawke,' I said. 'I told her she could leave, but it doesn't seem like she's in a mood to do that.'

Hawke sighed. 'Yeah, well, Mama can get like that.'

I just nodded, thinking that to say anything at this point would probably just sound rude.

MARY ELLEN

Mary Ellen sat in Emmett Hopkins's office and stared at the wall. If she was thinking of anything, it was at too low a note to be recorded here.

HOLLY

After the sheriff left the room, Holly was able to gather her wits about her to some extent. She stopped crying and took the tissue offered by the sheriff's wife, using it to wipe her eyes and blow her nose. She felt like an idiot. But if she thought about her laptop, she got all weepy again so she had to just push it out of her mind.

'I'm sorry,' she said to the sheriff's wife. 'I know it all seems silly, what with the boy being kidnapped and all, for me to be carrying on about my laptop, but . . .' She snuffled and blew her nose one more time.

'Not at all,' the sheriff's wife said. She smiled at Holly and Holly tried a tentative smile back. 'I'm Jean, by the way. My husband didn't introduce us.'

'Hi, Jean,' the girl said, sticking out her hand, 'I'm Holly.'

'Is it OK if I ask you a couple of questions? I'll leave all the stuff about "Mr Smith" to the sheriff. Right now we'll just focus on girl talk. Is that OK?'

Holly nodded her head. 'Sure,' she said.

'How old are you, Holly?' Jean asked.

'I'll be twenty-three next month. But I can play older – or younger.'

'So, you're an actress! What parts have you had?' Jean asked.

'Well, I was Rita's stand-in in *Educating Rita* in our high-school production,' Holly said, her chest swelling with pride.

'Wow,' Jean said. 'That's a tough role! "Rita" is on stage almost the entire time.'

'Yes, I know! That's a role you can really sink your teeth into.' Holly said, smiling brightly.

'How often did you get to do it?' the sheriff's wife asked.

Holly's face fell. 'Well, I didn't, not exactly. The play ran for two weekends, two Fridays and two Saturdays, and the second Saturday, Nanette Michelson, the one who was playing Rita, was like twenty minutes late and I thought, "Tonight's the night!" But then she showed up.'

'Oh,' Jean said. 'That's tough.'

Holly brightened. 'But I did get to play Juliet in a class production. It was mostly just reading from our seats in drama class, but Mr Clyde, the teacher, said I was *very* good.'

Then the door opened and the sheriff came back in. Holly straightened in her seat, hands clasped on the chipped and graffiti-marred table in front of her, and kept her mouth shut.

MILT

After listening in to Jean's gentle questioning of Holly Humphries, I came to the following conclusion: Holly Humphries calling herself an actress is like me calling myself a writer 'cause I write a mean grocery list.

I sat down across from the two women. 'OK, Miz Holly, I'm glad you're feeling better.' The girl nodded her head at me. 'Now, you called a number "Mr Smith" left on "Craig's List", is that right?'

'No, an email address,' she corrected.

'OK, you replied to his ad by sending an email,' I said. She nodded. 'Then what?'

'I gave him my cell phone number when I emailed him, and then he called my cell phone.'

'OK, great,' I said. 'Then what?'

'He asked me to meet him at a diner and I did,' Holly said.

'You remember the name of the diner?'

'Yes, it was Karla's Kitchen on Third Street down by the Goodwill.'

'Was that your pick or his?' I asked her.

'You mean Karla's Kitchen?' she asked. I nodded my head. 'You mean as a meeting place?' Again, I nodded my head. She thought about it for what seemed a fairly long time. 'I think it was his idea,' she said, staring off into space. 'But I can't really be sure. I mean, it's not like I'd never been there before. They have real cheap lunch specials. The food's not good, but you get a lot for like $3.99. Sometimes me and a friend would go in there and split it.'

'But you think it was his choice? To meet at Karla's Kitchen?' I said.

'Coulda been,' she said.

'What happened when you met there?' I asked.

'He looked at my résumé and then told me about the gig . . .'

'What did he say the, ah, gig was?' I asked.

'He said it was a documentary on safety to be shown to schoolchildren,' she said.

'Stranger danger,' I said.

'Huh?' Holly said.

'Never mind,' I said. 'Please, go on.'

'He told me it was going to be filmed on location, that all my expenses would be paid, and that I'd get an additional $500.' She looked up at me between long lashes. 'I don't guess I'm gonna get that $500 now, huh?'

I swear to God at that moment all I wanted to do was reach in my back pocket and give her all the cash there was in my wallet. But then, my wife was sorta sitting there. That'll curb those impulses.

ELEVEN

MILT

Holly Humphries told me her story, backtracking here and there, getting some things wrong and needing to correct them, remembering halfway through the story something she shoulda said at the very beginning, and me having to ask a hell of a lot of questions to get any kind of cohesive statement out of her. My main point of interest was where Emil Hawthorne had kept her and Eli the whole time.

'It was just a barn,' she said for the fourth time.

'What color was it?' I asked. Again.

She shrugged. 'Barn-colored?'

'Red? Natural wood? Pink with purple polka dots?'

'Milt . . .' Jean said.

I sighed. 'Can you do better than "barn-colored"?' I asked.

'Well, mostly wood-colored but I think there was some red in there. Like it had peeled and faded off mostly?' she suggested.

'Can you remember how long you drove and from where?' I asked.

'Well, we drove from Tulsa,' she said, looking at me like I was a total idiot, 'and it took a real long time.'

'Did you go through a town on your way to the barn?'

Holly thought about it. 'Nooooo, I don't think so.'

'Like with buildings, and red lights and stop signs?' I asked, getting a little testy.

She shook her head. 'No. No red lights. We passed some stop signs, though. At least, I remember stopping. He had me in the back most of the time doing stuff for him,' she said.

'Doing what stuff?' I demanded.

'Rolling up ropes neatly, and making sure stuff was secured on the walls of the van.'

'What stuff?' I asked.

'Oh, I dunno. You know, like duct tape, and screwdrivers, and a hammer, and a little hatchet thingy, and stuff like that,' Holly said.

'OK, so tell me about the barn,' I said.

She shrugged. 'It was a barn. I don't know much about barns. It seemed kinda big to me. There were hay bales in it, and he expected me to actually sit on one of them!' She shuddered at the thought. 'They were really itchy!'

'When you left the barn – when you and Eli ran off – what did you see?' I asked.

'Trees. Lots of trees. I mean, it was night-time, you know? Who could see? There was a driveway to the barn, and we tried to get to it, but Mr Smith caught us with his flashlight, and we ran back into the trees.'

'Tell me about Mr Smith,' Jean said, and I shot her a look.

The girl looked at Jean and widened her eyes. 'What about him?'

'His demeanor . . . how he acted. Angry, purposeful . . .' Jean tried.

'Oh, he was angry all right. All the time. Mad about everything! He yelled at me constantly, and then when he brought poor little Eli in . . . well, he didn't bring him in, I did,' Holly said.

I put up my hand to stop any further questions from my wife. This one I needed to field myself. '*You* brought Eli in? How do you mean?'

'Oh, Mr Smith had him in his van, and he told me to go get him out and like pull him into the barn, like I was his captor. And he filmed it.'

'He *filmed* it?' I repeated.

'Yes!' Holly said, drawing the word out to four or five syllables. 'I told you he told me he was a film director and I *thought* we were making a movie!'

'Excuse me,' I said and left the room. The girl was getting on my last nerve, and I had something I needed to do anyway. I found Emmett.

'Get the county map and check out the area for barns. Old ones. Think we can borrow that helicopter from Tulsa again?'

'No harm in asking,' Emmett said.

Then I walked down the hall to my office. I had me a deputy to interview. And I wasn't looking forward to it.

DALTON

Dalton blushed blood-red when the sheriff walked in, even though he hadn't been exploring the sheriff's office in over fifteen minutes. There just hadn't been that much to see, although it had all been fascinating to Dalton. All the paperwork the sheriff had to fill out, all the forms, and then there'd been the personnel files, where he found out Anthony Dobbins, who'd been hired a good ten years after Dalton, was getting paid a lot more than him. Dalton was thinking that wasn't fair, but he figured he needed to think on it some more.

'Hey, Dalton,' the sheriff said, and went and sat down in his chair behind his desk, which Dalton had luckily vacated when he finished going through the drawers.

'Hey, Milt,' he replied. 'Everybody OK out there?'

'Everybody's fine,' the sheriff answered.

'That girl Holly OK? You know, she didn't do nothing, Milt. She was just a . . . a pawn in that man Smith's scheme.'

The sheriff nodded his head. 'Dalton, I'm not gonna ask you where you were this weekend, or why you lied to your mama about it. That's your business. I just wanna know what happened when you met up with Holly Humphries and Eli, how that came about.'

Dalton blushed even harder, as impossible as that would seem, at the mention of his weekend and lying to his mama. 'Ah, well, I was in Tulsa and Mary Ellen had to come get me, and while she was driving us home, I fell asleep and she sorta got off track, I guess, lost, I guess, and when I woke up, she was gone and the car was dead, and I didn't know where I was. Didn't know we were right there at the falls. And I started wandering around, and then I met up with that girl Holly and she had Eli with her,' he said, all in a rush with hardly a breath in between.

'Did you see this Smith character?' the sheriff asked him.

Dalton shook his head vehemently. 'No, Sir! I did not.'

'Anything you can tell me about your nephew's kidnapping?'

'No, Sir!' Dalton said, sitting up at attention, feeling like he should stand and salute.

The sheriff stood up and headed for the door. 'Don't go anywhere,' he said and left the room.

MILT

Getting about as much out of Dalton as I figured I would, I left him sitting in my office and went next door to Emmett's office, where I'd had Dalton stash his sister, Mary Ellen.

I knocked and opened the door. She was sitting in a visitor's chair, staring at a framed award on Emmett's wall. Somehow, I figured she wasn't actually seeing it.

'Miz Knight?' I asked her.

She didn't start, just slowly turned her head to look at me. Her expression didn't change. 'Yes?' she said.

I slid in behind Emmett's desk and took a seat in his chair. 'Need to ask you a few questions,' I said to her. She didn't respond. 'Can you tell me where you went after you left Eli with Jean, my wife?'

'Tulsa,' she said.

'Why'd you do that?' I asked.

'Dalton called me.'

'Why?' I asked. She shrugged in response, but didn't say anything. 'Did he tell you why he wanted you to come to Tulsa?'

'Said he was in trouble,' she said. Her eyes, which had mostly been looking at my left ear, moved to stare again at Emmett's framed award.

'Ma'am?' I said. 'Could you look at me, please?'

Mary Ellen Knight turned her head slightly, her eyes tracking slower than her head.

'So, Dalton said he was in trouble and asked you to come get him in Tulsa. So you left Eli with Jean and you drove to Tulsa and got Dalton, right?' I said.

'No,' she said.

I shook my head like one of the Three Stooges. 'You just said that's what you did.'

'I didn't get Dalton. Not right away.'

OK, I thought. Here we go! She's talking. Two whole sentences! 'Why not?' I asked.

'He wasn't there,' she said, her fascination with my left ear back on.

'Where was he?' I asked.

She shrugged, and as she did, her eyes left my ear and traveled back to the framed award.

'Ma'am?' I said, and snapped my fingers toward her face. Her head turned slowly again, and her eyes made contact with my ear.

'Mary Ellen,' I said softly, 'is there *anything* you can tell me?'

Miracle of miracles, her eyes left my ear and actually looked directly into my eyes. 'No,' she said and then drifted back to the wall.

I got up and left the room, going back into the interrogation room, where my wife was still sitting with Holly Humphries. Opening the door, I motioned for Jean to join me outside.

I waited in the hall until she came out. 'What?' she asked.

'I think there's something wrong with Mary Ellen Knight,' I told her. 'Something *your* kinda wrong.'

'She seemed a little depressed when I talked with her at the birthday party yesterday,' Jean said.

'Well, I'm not a doctor like you are, but if what I saw was depression, then God help us all. She's in Emmett's office. Would you go see her?'

'Of course,' Jean said. Then she added, 'If you're going back in there with Holly, go easy. The girl really doesn't know anything, Milt.'

'She was just a pawn in Mr Smith's game, is that what you're saying?' I said, quoting Dalton.

My wife just looked at me, then said, 'If you're into the melodramatic, I'd have to agree.'

I headed back into the interrogation room.

HOLLY

Holly liked talking to Jean, the sheriff's wife. She was a nice lady, and real pretty, which made it a shame, Holly thought, that she was crippled and all.

She couldn't help wondering, sitting there all this time, what was happening to Eli. He was such a good little boy, really. She wanted to have kids some day, and if she did, she decided, she'd want a son just like Eli – but without the asthma. That, she felt, was a real pain in the ass. Holly liked things simple. She'd had enough complications in her own young life. Having to carry around something to help you breathe, or walk on crutches, like the sheriff's wife, was just more than she could bear to think of.

As Holly sat in the interrogation room of the sheriff's office, waiting for yet another drill by the sheriff, she had to wonder where her life would take her from this place. Back to Tulsa? Maybe. Maybe not. Tulsa seemed to be a bit of a dead end for Holly. Holly decided she needed new horizons. She just didn't know where they were.

TWELVE

CHARLIE

Charlie checked his computer access to city hall records and found a marriage license issued to Kevin Holcomb and Carolina Canfield on May 12, 2003. He also checked for domestic disturbances at the address in the Meadowbrook subdivision. There were none. Checking DMV records for former addresses on Kevin Holcomb, he found one at an address he knew was The Swallows, the nicest apartment complex out of the three in Longbranch. Police had been called to a domestic there on January 20, 2006. Neighbors had called in the complaint. A woman on the scene had bruises on her right arm and there was a broken dining-room chair. The woman said she bruised herself when she fell over the chair. She claimed the people who called in lived below them and complained if they walked too hard. No charges were brought.

Charlie looked at Milt's file on Albert Canfield, wishing he had information on the domestic file mentioned in 1983.

What were the chances, Charlie thought. Mother and daughter both abused, maybe, and both their husbands dying when they mixed the same damned chemicals? Zero. Zip. Those were the chances, Charlie thought. This was murder.

Carolina Canfield Holcomb had killed her husband, just like dear old mom.

MILT

There were no hits on AFIS on Holly Humphries. All we could confirm was that she had been in the Oklahoma Foster Care System, had aged out five years before, and had held a series of minimum-wage jobs, only one of which had required her to be fingerprinted, which had put her in *our* system.

I went back into the interrogation room. 'Miz Humphries,' I said, and she looked up. 'I want to thank you for co-operating with us in this investigation. I don't have any more questions for you at this moment, but I need you to stay in town if you can. Do you have any place to stay?'

The girl shook her head. 'No, Sir, and I don't have any money. Or anything. My purse and all my stuff are still in that barn. So if y'all find it, could you get my stuff for me?'

'Sure thing,' I said. 'Meanwhile, why don't I have my wife take you to the Wal-Mart and get some essentials, all on the county, of course, and then take you to a motel to stay until we get this all figured out.'

'Really?' Holly said, standing up, a smile lighting up her face something fierce. I gotta admit, she was a real pretty girl when she smiled.

I smiled back. 'Yes, Ma'am,' I said. 'You're gonna need a change of clothes,' I said. Then added, 'Or two.'

I thought that if the circumstances hadn't been as grim as they were, the young lady would have jumped up and down with joy.

I went back out front to talk to Jean, who was just coming out of Emmett's office. She pulled me down the hall, toward the side door that only sheriff's personnel used, as it was the only place right now, besides the jail cells, that wasn't jam-packed with people.

'Milt, I need to get Mary Ellen admitted to the hospital. She's close to a catatonic state. She needs medication immediately.'

I nodded my head and escorted my wife back out to the

big area, where Clovis Pettigrew and Rodney Knight sat. Both of the other children had gone with their brother into the kitchen to be fussed over by Gladys.

'Mr Knight,' Jean said, 'I've been talking with your wife, and I'm afraid there's a very big problem. I believe Mary Ellen is bipolar and at the moment she's in a deep depressive state. Unfortunately, there does appear to be some suicidal ideation . . .'

Little Clovis Pettigrew jumped to her feet. 'What is this nonsense?' she demanded. 'There is nothing wrong with my daughter! She needs a good night's sleep is all!'

'Mr Knight,' Jean said, trying like hell to ignore the mother, 'I highly recommend a thirty-day commitment to the hospital. She needs medication and therapy—'

'She needs sleep! If doofus here ever took care of the children for more than twenty minutes, maybe my girl could get some rest!' Clovis all but shouted. 'I told her and told her she shouldn'ta married you, but would she listen? Hell, no!'

'Miz Pettigrew,' I said, taking her by the arm, 'Dalton wants to talk to you.' I led her back to my office, where Dalton still sat in one of my two visitor chairs. I opened the door and handed Clovis Pettigrew inside. 'Dalton, your mama wants to talk to you,' I said, and shut the door.

Back in the big room, Gladys was busy receiving faxes and giving them to my wife, who was handing them over to Rodney Knight to sign. I heard the side door open and looked down the hall to see two EMTs coming in with a wheelchair. Even on crutches, when my wife moves, she *moves*.

'Can she say bye to the children?' Rodney asked, a tear in his eye.

'I think that would be a good idea,' Jean said. She went to Emmett's office and brought Mary Ellen out, while Gladys went to the kitchen area to bring out Mary Ellen's three children.

I took that moment to go check out what was inside Emmett's office, as I'm not real big on emotional scenes like that. By the time I came out, Mary Ellen and the EMTs were gone and Rodney Knight was packing up his children to take them home.

'Sheriff,' he said, 'my car's still at your house. If I could get a ride . . .' He looked down the hall toward my office, where his mother-in-law was currently, one could only assume, reading the riot act to her youngest.

Jean picked up her purse. 'I have my car here. I'll take you to the house. Rodney, Jr can use my son's car seat.'

'Thank you so much,' Rodney said, hurrying his children out the door.

Jean had barely started her car when Clovis Pettigrew came out of my office and down the hall toward me. I could see no escape.

'Where's my daughter?' she demanded.

'At the hospital. Her husband had her committed for thirty days . . .'

'Well, I'll put a stop to that!' she said, rushing toward the front door.

I caught her arm. 'Miz Pettigrew, stop just a damn minute!' I said.

She stopped all right. Then she turned to face me, looked first at my hand on her arm, and then stared daggers at me. 'If you let go of me right now, Sheriff, I won't press charges,' she said in a very tight voice.

I let go. 'Look, Ma'am, you gotta let Rodney do what's right for his wife . . .'

'That doofus wouldn't know what's right from what's left! He's as stupid as a bag of rocks—'

'Clovis Marie!' came a voice from behind me, and Miz Pettigrew and I both turned. Gladys was standing there with her arms across her chest, and that do-or-die look on her face was directed at Clovis and not at me. Thank the Lord.

'For once in your life, let it go! This is not your fault. You've done everything you could to raise these children up good and right. And you've done a bang-up job of it. Threepee was a fool for leaving you, and you and I both know it. But you did better without him than you ever would have with him. Now trust your children, trust yourself. Mary Ellen's having a hard time. It's not you. It's not Rodney. It's not the kids. It's something chemical in her brain. That's what clinical depression is. I should know, I've been on antidepressants for the last ten years, and thank God for 'em, is all I can say. Let Dr Jean do what she knows how to do, Clovis. Thirty days in the hospital will give Mary Ellen the rest she needs, the medication she needs and the therapy she needs to learn how to handle her depression. This is not your fault!'

There was a minute's silence, then Clovis Pettigrew burst into tears, something I would never have thought possible. Gladys went up to her and put her arms around her and walked her back to the kitchen, just as Dalton came out of my office.

'Did I hear my mama out here?' he asked.

'She's in the kitchen with Gladys, talking girl talk. Best leave 'em be. You OK?' I asked.

'Yes, Sir,' Dalton said. 'Mama's pretty pissed, though.'

'Yeah, I figured as much.' Then I had my brainstorm. 'You're on duty now, right?'

'Yes, Sir,' Dalton said.

'Well, I've got an assignment for you.'

HOLLY

Holly had never been in a police car for any reason before, but it was nice that her first ride in one was for a trip to Wal-Mart and not to jail. It's not like Holly had never done anything illegal – she had shoplifted once in high school and had smoked marijuana when she was with Joshua. She'd also broken into a defunct amusement park in the middle of the night with some of her girlfriends and tried to ride rides that wouldn't work without electricity. For a drunken stunt, it hadn't been a lot of fun. It was actually so boring that one girl sobered up.

But for all of her felonies and misdemeanors, she had never been caught; thus, she had never ridden in a police car.

Dalton was really quiet on the way to the Wal-Mart, which was out on the highway, away from the town of Longbranch, which she had yet to see. He parked close to the front and got out, still not saying a word.

A little disgusted, Holly said, 'You don't have to go in with me.'

'Yes, Ma'am,' he said. 'I gotta. Need to pay.'

Holly got a cart and headed first to the health and beauty section. She needed the works: deodorant, shampoo and conditioner, a hair brush, and hairdryer, toothbrush and toothpaste, floss and mouthwash (one of the 'dads' in one of her foster families had been a dentist), body conditioner, soap, a pair of nail clippers and a package of emery boards, and she gave herself a little present of a knock-off bottle of the perfume, Obsession.

Dalton just walked along, not saying a word, mostly looking away whenever she put anything in the cart, as if her purchases embarrassed him. Holly thought about throwing in a box of tampons to really embarrass him, but knowing she was nowhere near her period, she decided not to charge the county for that particular non-necessity.

'I need to go to the clothes now,' Holly told Dalton.

''Kay,' he said, and followed along silently.

All the clothes she now had were the jeans and T-shirt she was wearing, along with the flip-flops that hadn't been a big help while running through the forest, thank you very much. She also had on a bra and panties, but she'd been wearing them for so long, she thought they were probably expendable. So she headed first to the lingerie section, noticing that Dalton didn't even follow her off the tile and onto the carpet. He just stayed in the main aisle, looking off toward housewares. She bought a package of three different-colored cotton bikini panties, a new bra, and then headed for the good stuff.

If truth be known, Holly loved clothes. She just never had the money to buy any. She did all of her shopping at thrift stores, and usually only bought things like deodorant and stuff at places like Wal-Mart. The last time she'd had clothes from Wal-Mart was during the short period she worked for them, when she got a 10 per cent discount. So she took her time, looking at the pants and tops and even dresses and skirts hanging on the racks.

When she caught Dalton looking at a pretty, silk-looking

top, she said, 'Hey, that's nice.' She walked up to him,
noticing the red infusing his face. 'What size is it?' she
asked.

'Dunno,' he said, turning redder, his hand off the top and
in his pockets.

Holly took the top off the rack, saw it was actually her size,
and turned to smile at Dalton. 'Hey, it's my size!' She held it
up in front of her, close to her body. 'What do you think?'

'It's OK,' he said and turned away.

Upset, Holly put the top back on the shelf. She'd already
found two bottoms in her size – another pair of jeans and
some khaki Bermuda shorts – and two tops – a baby-doll
sleeveless top in light blue, and a short-sleeved camp shirt
in white.

'OK, I'm ready to check out,' she told Dalton.

'Ah, you wanna get a dress or something?' Dalton
suggested.

'Why?' she asked.

His faced turned crimson again and he looked away from
her. 'Don't know how long you're gonna have to be here.
Might have to go out to dinner or something,' he said.

Holly looked at Dalton and smiled. He didn't see it,
though, as he wasn't looking her way. So, she thought, he's
gonna ask me out to dinner. Then she sighed. OK, *I'm*
gonna have to ask *him* out. Whatever.

They headed for the dresses, with Holly's mind already
thinking, Shoes!

MILT

Me and Emmett drove out to a barn on a piece of land that
had been foreclosed on almost a year before, figuring that
barn should be pretty beat up. There was nothing there. No
evidence that Emil Hawthorne had ever held hostages at
this location.

We were back in Emmett's car, heading to a second
location, when we got a call from Anthony Dobbins.

'Sheriff?'

'Yeah, Anthony?'

'We got a DB over at Mitch Dovey's place on the back side of Mountain Falls. Some trespassing hikers found it.'

'Who the hell is it?' I asked.

'Well, Sir, the ID in his pocket says it's Emil Hawthorne.'

We hightailed it back toward my house. You had to take a road off Highway-5, go up the mountain a ways, on the other side of the mountain from my house, then there was a turnoff to Mitch Dovey's spread. He never did live there, but he used to grow about 100 acres of cotton there every year, until he got too old to care. The 100 acres was shielded from the side road by old oaks and pines and what have you, and most of the former cotton fields were overgrown now with second-growth trees and wild grasses. But at the back of the spread, he had an old barn, nestled in some trees up against the foothills.

The body was lying in front of the barn. I got out of Emmett's car and walked up to where Anthony Dobbins was standing. 'You call it in to Doc Church?' I asked, naming the new county medical examiner.

'Yes, Sir,' Anthony said. He handed me a wallet. There was a newly minted Illinois driver's license, a Visa card, an American Express card and around $400 in cash. The ID and both credit cards carried the name 'Emil Hawthorne' big as all get out. The DB was lying on his stomach, his face in the ground. What blood there was came from the head area.

'You see where he was shot?' I asked Anthony.

'Yes, Sir. Two shots. One right between the eyes, and another in the left cheek area. But by the amount of blood, I'd say the first shot got him. Figuring the one between the eyes.'

'How so?' I asked.

'Well, Sir, the shooter would be aiming real good the first time, and the second shot would just be like overkill.' He stopped for a minute, grinned sheepishly, and said, 'No pun intended, Sir.'

I grinned back. 'You might wanna remember it, though,' I said, 'in case this scenario ever comes up again.'

'Yes, Sir, copy that,' Anthony said.

We heard a car pulling into the long driveway and waited while the ME parked and got out. Rose Church was elected shortly after Old Doc Watson had retired. She was usually an anesthesiologist, but she was still good at pointing out that somebody was dead. Me and her didn't get along real good, but that was neither here nor there.

'Hey, Dr Church,' I said as she walked up to the DB.

'Hey yourself, Sheriff,' she said. 'How're Jean and your boy?'

Well, that story was so long I didn't dare get into it, so I just said, 'Fine, thanks for asking.'

'Who we got here?' she asked, nudging the dead body with the toe of her shoe.

Dr Church was a mannish-looking woman, with real short salt-and-pepper hair, a body like a fireplug and big hands for a woman. But then, who am I to say? Saying such a thing out loud would just get me in trouble with somebody.

'A foreigner,' I said. 'From Chicago.'

'Humph,' she said at my attempted humor.

With Anthony's help, she turned the body over. There appeared to be no wounds other than the two shots to the face. He was a skinny guy, with gray hair and a sallow complexion. I'm not sure if that was from the coma or newly developed due to him being dead and all.

Dr Church took out a hand-held recorder and began to speak into it. 'Two gunshot wounds, look like twenty-two caliber, one between the eyes, the other center of the left cheek. No other wounds visible. By the lack of blood, I'd say fairly instantaneous death.' She turned off the recorder and rolled the body back over onto its stomach. Pointing at the back of his head, she said, 'Birds have been pecking on him pretty good back here, so no telling how long he's been laying here. I'll have to take him in to figure out time of death, but off the top of my head, I'd say, he's already gone through rigor, which means he's been laying here for at least six hours,' Dr Church said.

At least six hours. Emmett had found the hostages no more than four hours ago. Seemed like I needed to have me another talk with sweet little Miz Holly Humphries.

DALTON

Dalton had made the executive decision to take Holly Humphries to the Longbranch Inn rather than to the Motel Five out on Highway-5. For some reason he couldn't fathom, he wanted Holly to like his hometown, and there was nothing much out on Highway-5 to like. But the Longbranch Inn sat right on the square, right across from the county courthouse, and was real old and real pretty and the rooms were made up old-fashioned-like and he thought she might like it. Not that he cared, but it was nice to be nice to someone who'd been through what she'd been through. Not to mention how she probably saved his nephew's life.

Coming into town on Highway-5, Dalton said, 'This here Highway Five turns into Main Street right here. That over there is the post office. The original one. Well, not really. The original one was a shack, but this is the second original one.'

'Very nice,' Holly said, staring at the Georgian-style brick building with the mismatched shingles on the roof.

'That there in the middle of the square,' he said, pointing straight ahead of them, 'is the courthouse. It's real old, too.'

'It looks real old,' Holly agreed. 'But very pretty.'

'County had it refurbished 'bout five years ago,' Dalton said proudly.

'That must be why it looks so good,' Holly said.

'Yeah. Across the street there,' he said, pointing, 'is the Longbranch Inn. That's where you'll be staying. They got the best food in town. And real nice rooms. Our head deputy Emmett Hopkins and his wife Jasmine, who's also a deputy, they spent their wedding night there,' he said, then blushed bloodred.

'I'm sure I'm gonna like it just fine,' Holly assured him.

'Dalton come in,' came over the radio.

Dalton picked up the mic and switched it on. 'Car Three, over,' he said.

'It's Milt. Miss Humphries still there with you?'

'Yes, Sir, over,' Dalton said.

'Bring her on back here, would'ja please?'

'Before or after I check her in at the hotel, over,' Dalton said.

'Right now means right now, Dalton. Oh, and over and out,' Milt said and hung up.

HOLLY

Holly liked that Dalton had started talking, and liked the way he talked about his hometown. She guessed Tulsa was her hometown, but she didn't feel that way about it. The little parts of the city she knew she wasn't really keen on. But when Dalton brought her to the downtown area of Longbranch, she could certainly see why he was prideful about his hometown. It was beautiful. Just like out of a movie – maybe a Western, but still and all. The courthouse in the middle of town was surrounded by centuries-old oak trees, and the lawn was green and perfect, with spring flowers bursting forth all over. Each little store had a big old pot in front of it with spring flowers. The hotel he pointed out was almost as ornate as the courthouse, and she couldn't wait to see her room in such a place.

But then the call came in from the sheriff, and Dalton turned the squad car around, heading back out Highway-5 to the sheriff's department. She didn't like the feel of this at all.

Once there, Dalton parked on the side, and led her in through the staff-only entrance. Normally, she would have found that fairly cool, but right now she was a little upset. She really wanted to rest, to lay down in what she knew would be a four-foot-high four-poster bed in a room with old-fashioned wallpaper, and close her eyes to sweet dreams about cowboys and dancehall queens.

The sheriff was in his office, the first door they came to. He looked up. 'Hey, Miz Humphries, come on in.' He stood up and ushered her to a chair. 'Thanks, Dalton, please close the door behind you.'

And then she was alone with the sheriff.

'Miz Humphries, I need to ask you a few questions,' the sheriff said.

'Yes, Sir,' she said. 'I think I told you everything, but anything you need.'

'When exactly was the last time you saw the man you say you knew as Mr Smith?'

Not being a complete and total idiot, Holly didn't miss 'the man *you say* you knew as Mr Smith.' That sounded as if he didn't believe her, and if he didn't believe her, what was she going to do? Holly took a deep breath and then plunged ahead. 'That's the only way I knew him, Sheriff, I swear to God. He told me his name was Mr Smith. He never said anything else. No first name, no nothing. I shoulda asked, I know, but I was so happy to get an acting gig that I just took him at his word!'

The sheriff nodded his head. 'OK,' he said. 'But I still need to know, when exactly was the last time you saw him?'

'Oh, yeah. OK. Uh.' Holly thought for a moment, then said, 'As Eli and I were running away. It was dark, I guess last night some time, and we were running along the woods near the driveway, and he shone his flashlight on us and we ran back into the thick woods behind the barn.' Another bout of thinking, then she said, 'At least, I think it was Mr Smith. I didn't see his face, just the flashlight beam, but who else could it have been?'

'Who else, indeed?' the sheriff said ominously. 'Let's go over again how you met Mr Smith.'

So Holly painstakingly described yet again how she'd seen the ad on 'Craig's List' and had emailed the address listed and how Mr Smith had called her and set up a meet. She told the sheriff every last detail of every encounter she'd had with Smith, then asked, 'Do I need a lawyer?'

'Why would you need a lawyer?' the sheriff asked.

'I don't know,' Holly said, tears building up behind her eyes and her voice getting wet. 'You're scaring me!' she wailed and burst into tears.

At which point, the sheriff's door opened and Dalton Pettigrew burst in.

'What'd you do to her?' he yelled at the sheriff.

Through tear-filled eyes, she saw the sheriff stand up and walk around his desk. She turned to look up at Dalton, her eyes pleading.

'Let's you and me go outside, Deputy,' the sheriff said,

and they closed the door, leaving Holly alone in the sheriff's office.

MILT

I grabbed Dalton by the arm and dragged him down the hall to the now-empty lobby. 'What the hell did you think you were doing?' I demanded.

'She didn't have nothing to do with this, Milt!' Dalton said, for all the world looking like he could punch me out. I'd never seen that look on Dalton's face before, and I must say, if you'll excuse the expression, I was nonplussed.

'You don't know that, Dalton. And I'm not saying that she did. But I got some tough questions to ask, and she's one of the people I need to ask them to. She's the only one who knew Smith, she came here *with* Smith . . .'

'And she saved Eli's life!' Dalton all but shouted.

'No doubt she did,' I said. 'Maybe she changed her mind about being in on it, or maybe she didn't know anything about it. I don't know. All I do know is that Dr Church says Smith's been dead like six hours. And y'all were found four hours ago. Seems like there's leeway for Holly to have shot Smith and left with Eli.'

'Don't you think Eli would have noticed if she'd shot Mr Smith?' Dalton demanded.

Hum, I thought. He had me there. 'Maybe she did it while he was asleep. Or maybe she'd already run away with Eli, left him stashed in the woods, then come back and did Smith.'

'That's stupid!' Dalton said.

I looked at him hard and he said, 'Sir.'

'You go swab out the cells right now, Dalton. And don't come down my hallway until I call for you. You got that?' I said.

He stared at me hard for a minute and then said, grudgingly, 'Yes, Sir,' and headed for the broom closet to get the cleaning supplies for the jail cells. They'd been cleaned on Saturday by Lonnie Sturgis and we hadn't had anyone in there since then, but it was a 'keep busy' kind of chore, and we both knew it.

I went back to my office, where Holly Humphries was blowing her nose and drying her eyes. I sat down behind my desk and said, 'Miz Humphries, I'm not accusing you of anything, and if you want a lawyer, you can call one.'

'I don't know any lawyers,' she said, a sob in her voice.

'I'll call one for you, if you want me to. But I'm not accusing you of anything. I'm just trying to find out what we can about this Mr Smith. And what happened after you and Eli left him. You see, Miz Humphries, somebody shot Mr Smith about the same time you say you got away from him. Shot him twice in the face. Killed him dead.'

Holly's eyes got huge and her mouth quivered. 'I swear to God I didn't kill him, Sheriff.'

'It'd be best if we could prove that, Holly. How 'bout we do a paraffin test? Check your hands for gunshot residue?'

She held her hands out toward me. 'I've never shot a gun in my life, Sheriff. Have at it. Can I take a polygraph, too?' she said, beginning to lose her fear and getting a little excited. 'And you can swab my mouth for DNA!'

I grinned. 'Watch a little *CSI*, do you?' I asked.

She grinned back. 'All three of them! I think they should set one down here. Though they'd probably put it in Houston. But that would be OK, don'ja think?'

'Hate Houston,' I told her, getting out the kit to do the gunshot residue test. 'Maybe New Orleans?'

'Oh, hey!' she said, all excited. 'That would be great! Never thought of that!'

'Did you ever see Mr Smith talking on the phone with anyone? Here or in Tulsa? Talking to anyone on the street in Tulsa? Anything like that?'

Holly shook her head. 'No,' she said. 'He did have a cell phone, though. Did you find it?'

I shook my head while I swabbed her hands. 'No,' I said, 'he didn't have one on him. But speaking of finding things. We did find your purse and your knapsack. They're behind Gladys's desk.'

'Oh, wow, great!' Holly said. Then her face fell. 'But I already spent all that money at Wal-Mart.'

What can I say? This kid was a sweetheart. And her hands were clean, at least of gunshot residue. 'You're clean,' I told her, handing her a wipe to clean her hands. No way in hell was she involved with Smith. OK, maybe that was just wishful thinking, but still it was there. 'Don't worry about Wal-Mart,' I said. 'Our treat.'

Holly started to stand up then sat back down real quick. 'Can I go now?' she asked.

'Unless you can think of anything you haven't already told me,' I said.

I could actually see the girl thinking. 'Nooooo,' she said slowly. 'Nothing I can think of.'

'Well, you still need to stick around Prophesy County for a few days, so have Dalton take you on over to the Longbranch, get you checked in.'

She stood up and held out her hand, a smile on her face. 'Thanks, Sheriff. You've been really fair with me and I appreciate it.'

'Long as you tell me everything you know, Miz Humphries, no reason to get excited.'

She shook my hand, or rather pumped it, and said, 'Call me Holly.'

I nodded and she hightailed it out the door.

THIRTEEN

EMIL

It wouldn't have been a pleasant experience had Emil Hawthorne been alive. He was cut down the middle, his organs weighed and put in jars, the bullets excised from his head, and his body endured many more indignities. But such is death, and Emil Hawthorne was irrevocably dead.

MILT

Me and Emmett were in my office with Charlie Smith, discussing the late Emil Hawthorne. 'He had a cell phone Holly said,' I told them. 'But one wasn't found at the scene. Not even Holly's cell phone was found. She said Hawthorne confiscated it when he tied her and the boy up. So what happened to the cell phones?'

'Whoever shot him took 'em?' Charlie offered.

'Why both?' Emmett asked.

''Cause they didn't know which one was Hawthorne's?' I suggested.

'Don't they say the number on them somewhere?' Emmett asked.

Charlie and me both shrugged. 'But there would be a list of numbers that number called, right? That's how I find my wife's cell – I don't even know what her number is, I just scroll down through my phone until I find her name,' Charlie said.

'Yeah, and if Hawthorne was talking to whoever killed him, then that person's name or number would show up on the memory, right?' I asked.

'Sounds good,' Emmett said, and Charlie nodded his agreement.

'So maybe whoever shot him was in a hurry,' Charlie suggested. 'Didn't have time to stop and figure out which cell phone was Hawthorne's. Erred on the side of caution.'

Emmett and I nodded.

'So, Hawthorne wasn't alone in this,' I mused. 'But who would he be partnering with? I mean, the man was in a coma for eight years. How come all of a sudden he's got a partner? And who would partner up on what was basically a personal revenge thing against Jean?'

We all thought on that for a minute. Then Emmett said, 'OK, the man wakes up from a coma eight months ago. Let's say he spends, what, three or four months doing rehab. A lot of shit would atrophy in eight years, know what I mean? So we're saying two to three months to plan all this shit against Jean.'

'Yeah, first he's gotta find her,' I said.

'Not hard. She's an MD, Milt. It would take about two seconds to find her on the Internet,' Charlie said.

That made me a little queasy.

'Then he does the whole "Craig's List" thing and gets Holly. Probably didn't take that long. Has to get all the equipment he needs to pretend he's making a movie, and all the real stuff he'll need for the kidnapping,' Emmett said.

I made a slightly disgusted sound – OK a snort. 'So he did what he did. What good is a time line doing us?'

'Somewhere in there he met a confederate. How much time did he have to get someone to care about helping him with this thing? There was no money payoff—'

'Wait a second!' I said. I stood up and paced my small office, having to move Emmett's big feet to do so. 'When Jean was telling me about how she found out all that shit about Hawthorne, she said it all started when his pet intern from the term before showed up begging him for something. She said the girl was really hung up on him. So what if it wasn't a new confederate, but an old conquest?'

'Bingo,' Charlie said.

HOLLY

Dalton checked Holly in to the Longbranch Inn and then helped her carry her packages up to her room. The stuff recovered from the farmhouse, her backpack and purse, were both slung over Holly's shoulder. She hadn't recovered her cell phone. In fact, there was a good possibility that the killer had taken her cell phone, confusing it for Mr Smith's. Which, in a way, was exciting. But on the other hand, Holly thought, she could sure use her phone.

Dalton used the key the lady at the desk had given him and opened the door to room 214. Four was Holly's lucky number. She took this as a sign that things were going to get better for her. She snuck a peak at Dalton and kinda hoped that he would have something to do with things getting better.

She walked into the room and was dumbstruck. It was

almost exactly how she imagined. She could see Miss Kitty, that lady from those old *Gunsmoke* reruns on TV, sitting in this room waiting for Marshal Dillon to show up. It was indeed a four-poster bed, all carved with flowers and such, and it was indeed at least four feet off the ground. In fact, there was a little stool next to the side of the bed – a two-stepper for the lady of the room to use. The beautiful bedspread was a blue willow design, as was the wallpaper. She thought some might think it a little busy, but Holly thought it was classy and beautiful. There was even a dark wood hutch against the wall, carved with the same kind of flowers as the bed posts, and the glass doors showed blue willow patterned dishes – a platter and a soup tureen, and a beautifully shaped coffee server with little matching cups and saucers.

She turned and looked at Dalton and the look on her face was pure joy. He couldn't help but smile back.

JEAN

'Oh my God,' Jean said, when Milt came home with his theory. 'You really think it was one of his women?'

'I don't know, honey, but it's as good a place as any to start. Anyway, can you help me find out where some of those you talked to are now?' Milt asked.

'Let me get on the Internet, do some research,' Jean said, and headed for her office in their son's former nursery, leaving Milt to finish supper and get John settled. She wondered how Milt would manage to end up frying the salad she'd started for dinner, and smiled.

There was absolutely nothing on Greta Schwartzmann Nichols, but there was an entire website for Melinda Hayes, who was now Melinda Hayes Solomon. She was now a day trader and mommy of two, and even if she had a nanny, Jean couldn't see her following Emil Hawthorne to Oklahoma to help him wreak vengeance on an old colleague.

LeeLee Novotny had committed suicide three years ago. That information took Jean's breath away, and she had to sit for a while and contemplate her own guilt in LeeLee's demise. She'd done the best she could for the young woman, found her all the help she could find. Jean decided to lay blame where it belonged: at the feet of LeeLee's mother and Emil Hawthorne.

After searching the web for what seemed like, and was, hours, Jean finally gave up and went to bed, where Milt was already fast asleep and snoring.

The next morning, Jean called DeSandra and asked her to push back her nine o'clock appointment, telling her she'd be in late. Then, informing Milt he would be taking John to preschool, she sat down in her robe with a cup of coffee and resumed her search. The first search was of her own memory, then to her alma mater for a list of the medical school graduating class that she was in.

She wrote down three names of graduates who had gone on to be interns with her. Two had been in the psych rotation. And one of them, Jean was pretty sure, was the guy who had told the rest of the group of Greta's identity. His name was Eric Loeman and he hadn't gone into psychiatry. He was an oncologist now living in Houston and working at MD Anderson.

She found both his home and office number and dialed the office number first. A secretary answered and told her that the doctor was at the hospital and would be returning calls in the afternoon. Jean left a short message: 'Just tell him I was an intern with him in Chicago, and I need to speak with him urgently.' She gave her home and cell number and headed in to work.

DALTON

Dalton's job this Tuesday morning was to check on Holly Humphries and to keep tabs on her all day. That's what Milt said to do and that's exactly what Dalton intended to do. That it wasn't a terrible assignment did enter Dalton's mind, but he pushed it aside with the intention of doing his job without enjoying it.

He drove his squad car up to the Longbranch Inn and parked, getting out and going into the lobby and up to the desk. 'Hey, Mavis,' he said to the lady behind the desk, 'could you call up to Miz Humphries room and tell her I'm here, please?'

'Holly?' Mavis said. 'She's having breakfast in the dining room.'

'Thanks,' Dalton said and ambled into the dining room. The dining room, like the rooms upstairs, had been redone in the early 1990s, and it boasted a turn of the century (the *other* century) décor that included imitation gas lamps on the walls, flocked wallpaper and lacy-looking plastic table cloths. They hadn't bothered with the floor because they ran out of money after doing the rooms upstairs, and it was still the same linoleum tile that had been there since the last remodel in 1952.

It took Dalton a minute to find Holly in the large dining room, as almost every table was taken. The Longbranch Inn made a slam-bam breakfast, and that was a fact. Finally, he saw her in the corner by the stuffed five-point buck and headed her way. She looked up and saw him and smiled. He smiled back. He couldn't help himself. Besides, he was just being polite.

'Hey, Deputy!' Holly said. He noticed she was wearing those khaki short things from yesterday and the white shirt, and they looked really good with her coloring – her olive complexion and reddish brown hair and those green eyes that shimmered like emeralds under the lights of the hotel dining room. 'Join me?' Holly asked.

'Thanks,' Dalton said, his face turning red as he took a chair facing the dead deer. 'Sheriff said I was to be at your service today, Miz Humphries, so anything you wanna do . . .'

'Oh! Don't you have more important things to do?' she asked and then her face paled. 'Or does he still think I'm a suspect?' Tears sprang to her eyes and she put down her fork on the plate, her Longbranch Inn morning special – two eggs any way, ham, bacon and sausage, hash browns or grits and a choice of toast or a biscuit – totally forgotten.

'Oh, no, Ma'am!' Dalton said, willing to do anything to dry the tear in her eye. 'I think he's punishing me for causing so much trouble . . .'

'I'm your punishment?' Holly said, the tear not drying up a bit.

'Oh, no, Ma'am! I didn't mean that! The sheriff may think it's a punishment,' Dalton said, turning a magenta, 'but *I* sure don't think it is.'

'Oh,' Holly said, and smiled. Dalton smiled back. 'Why don't you call the waitress over and join me for breakfast, Deputy?'

'Sure thing, Ma'am, and you can call me Dalton,' he said.

JEAN

Jean arrived at the office and had half an hour before her next appointment. Anne Louise was also between patients, so they sat in the coffee room discussing the horrors of the past two days.

'I can't believe you had to go through all this, Jean. I'm so sorry,' Anne Louise said.

'Thank you. It's been an incredible experience. I'm just so thankful no one got hurt. I mean, none of the children or . . .'

Anne Louise reached across the table and patted Jean's hand. 'I know, honey. That louse Hawthorne's dead, but we're not counting him.'

'Did you know him, back in Chicago?' Jean asked her partner.

'Only by reputation,' Anne Louise said. 'He was a genius, they said.'

'He was,' Jean agreed. 'But so were Svengali and Machiavelli, and hell,' Jean said, laughing slightly, 'they say even Ted Bundy was smart.'

Patting Jean's hand again, Anne Louise said, 'Just try to put this out of your mind. For now, anyway. When you have time to get perspective on it, then we'll sit down for real and have a session, OK?'

Jean nodded. 'You're right,' she said. 'I need to just let it percolate.'

'Thatagirl,' Anne Louise said, standing up and hugging Jean. 'I've got some paperwork to do. We'll talk later?'

'You bet,' Jean said, and watched her friend walk out the door. Suddenly, she felt very lonely.

HOLLY

Holly was delightfully surprised to find out how much there was to see in Longbranch and the rest of Prophesy County. There were some cute boutiques and antique shops around the square in downtown Longbranch, and Dalton even took her up on Mountain Falls Road, where the sheriff lived. She could hardly believe this was just two miles from where she'd been held captive and where she and Eli had wandered in the woods like Moses and the lost tribe of Egypt. (One of her foster 'moms' was a lay preacher for an Evangelical church, and it was amazing how much she absorbed in what, thankfully, turned out to be a very short stay.)

'But we won't go to his house,' Dalton said. 'Nobody home and, anyway, I want to show you the falls. We never did get there the other night.'

They passed the sheriff's house and Dalton pointed down the long driveway. 'See it back there?' he said. 'White stucco with a flat roof?'

'Oh yeah!' Holly said. 'It looks like something you'd see in New Mexico or something.'

'Yeah, real exotic for this area,' Dalton said. 'But it's real nice inside.'

'I guess I'll have to take your word for that,' Holly said.

'Let me show you the falls,' he said, and started the car rolling down the hill.

They got to the bottom on the far side of Mountain Falls Road, and Dalton pulled into a large flat area. 'This used to be an RV park,' he told her. 'Until we had a real bad tornado and this whole area got flooded. It was really something.'

He got out of his car and walked around to open her door, but she'd already done that. They bumped into each other as she was getting out of the car.

'Oh, sorry—' Holly said, just as Dalton was saying, 'Sorry.' They both stood there for a few seconds, so close they were almost touching and then Dalton quickly backed up. 'Sorry, Ma'am.'

'No, that's OK,' Holly said. 'I'm just not used to guys opening doors for me. The guys in Tulsa, at least the ones I know, don't exactly have manners.'

'Well, that just proves they weren't raised right, Ma'am,' Dalton said.

There was an awkward silence and then Holly put on her super-cheerful voice and said, 'Now, where did you say those falls were?'

JEAN

Luckily, Jean wasn't with a patient when Eric Loeman, the oncologist from Houston, called her back.

'Hey, Jean?' he said when her got her on the phone. 'What the hell? I can't believe I'm hearing from you after all this time! How you doing?'

Jean wondered if he really remembered her or if he was just trying to be slick. She remembered him as being the slick type.

'I'm doing great, Eric. How are you?' she asked.

'Great, great. Head of my department here at Anderson. Married a Miss Texas runner-up. Got three kids. My oldest is going into medicine like his old man, and my daughter, well, if she ever gets through with all this beauty pageant business, I hope she'll get serious about a career!'

'The reason I called,' Jean said, breaking in before she had to hear about the wonderfully planned future of the third child, 'is about Emil Hawthorne.'

'Good God, haven't heard that name in a while. He still in a coma or did he finally die?' Eric said.

'Actually,' Jean said, 'he woke up from the coma—'

'Jesus H Christ on a bicycle! You serious? How long?'

'Eight years—'

'Mother Mary and Joseph! Can you beat that? So how's he doing? Got all his faculties? I mean, that would be a real shame for a guy like that to wake up and be stupid, know what I mean?'

'Ah, well, he seemed to have all his faculties, but he's dead now.'

'You just said—' Eric started.

'I know. He was fine for about six or seven months, then someone shot him.'

'No shit?' Eric said. 'Who?'

'We don't know,' Jean said. 'Eric, the reason I'm calling—'

'Who's *we*?' Eric asked.

'I'm sorry?'

'You said "*we* don't know". Who's *we*?'

'Oh,' Jean said. 'My husband and I. He's the sheriff for the county where Hawthorne was shot. Anyway, Eric, the reason—'

'You married a sheriff?' Eric demanded.

'Yes . . .'

'Where?'

'Where *what*?'

'Where is he the sheriff?'

Jean sighed. She'd forgotten what a prick Eric Loeman was. 'Prophesy County, Oklahoma. Now, Eric—'

'Oh, Jesus!' Eric said and laughed. 'You mean Baja Texas, don'ja? I can't believe you live in Oklahoma! You were so good! I thought you'd be in New York by now. You still in psychiatry?'

'Yes, I'm still in psychiatry. I run the hospital's psych wing here and have a private practice—'

'Bet you got a lot of nuts in Oklahoma, huh?' Eric said and laughed again.

'Eric,' Jean said, her voice a little more abrupt than she meant for it to be, 'I've got a patient in just a few minutes and I really need to ask you some questions. It's for the case.'

'No shit. Shoot!' Eric said.

'You remember that girl who had been Hawthorne's assistant before me? Greta Schwartzmann Nichols?'

'Oh, yeah! She was banging him. You didn't ever bang him, did you?' Eric asked.

'No, Eric, I didn't! Now, do you know where Greta might be now? I couldn't find her on the Internet . . .'

'That's 'cause she changed her name,' Eric said.

'She got married?' Jean inquired.

'So to speak. She's now Sister Mary something-or-other. Last I heard, she was working at some Catholic hospital somewhere.'

'You're not sure what her name is now?'

'No. Wish I could help you. Can't even swear that it's Mary something. Just that it's not Greta anymore.'

'Well, thank you so much, Eric—'

'Hey, it was great talking to you, Jean! We need to stay in touch. Give me your numbers—'

'Oh, damn, my patient's here! I've got your number, Eric. I'll give you a call!'

'Great—'

Jean hung up the phone.

HOLLY

It was beautiful. Oak and pine and other trees Holly didn't recognize surrounded a crystal-blue pool. She couldn't believe she'd been so close to this the other night, but then she figured, under the circumstances, she probably wouldn't have appreciated it the way she did now.

Large boulders rimmed the pool, some flat enough to sit on. What with spring rains and snow run-off, Mountain Falls Creek was swollen this year. The falls themselves, while certainly not Niagara quality, were running hard and fast, filling the pool to capacity and running off to the lower part of Mountain Falls Creek, which changed its name to Lazy Creek a half mile down.

Holly sat on the flat rock next to Dalton, their bodies almost touching. She was beginning to really like this big, slow-talking deputy. He had a sweetness she wasn't used to, and an old-fashioned way about him that made her feel like a lady, a feeling she usually only got when acting.

Wild flowers filled the grassy areas around the pool, and she saw Dalton lean down from the rock for a moment, then come back up with a daisy in his hand.

His face turning its usual red, he handed the flower to her without a word.

For the first time in her memory, Holly felt her face grow hot, and wondered if Dalton's condition was contagious. 'Thank you,' she said.

Dalton nodded his head.

Holly decided they needed to leave, right that minute. Because otherwise, she figured, in about two minutes she was going to jump his bones.

MILT

Jean called me with the information about Greta Schwartzmann Nichols. Looked like a dead end to me and I told her so.

'You forget I'm a Catholic in good standing, Milt,' she said. 'My dad and the Archbishop of the Chicago Diocese are golfing buddies. If Greta did take her vows, I'll find her.'

I shook my head. 'Babe, I don't doubt you for a minute,' I said. 'Call me when you can.'

We said some mushy stuff and then she hung up. I wandered into Emmett's office and sat down.

'Talk to me,' I said to my oldest friend and head deputy. 'Tell me what the hell's going on with our dead perv.'

Emmett leaned back in his chair, elbows out, hands clasped behind his head. 'Well, now, what do we have here? Jean discovers a doctor who's doing it with under-age patients and turns him in. He goes tooling off in his Corvette – ain't that always the way? Some dumb-ass doctor gets to buy a Corvette, and law-abiding peace officers such as ourselves get stuck with Jeeps and Tauruses? – Anyway, he wraps his Corvette, vintage I found out, around a tree or a lamp post or something, ends up in a coma for eight years and comes out of it like it was the next fucking day. Then decides he's going to seek revenge against the woman who turned him in and caused all his problems, as far as he's concerned. Am I up to speed so far?'

'Doing good,' I informed him.

'So he does his rehab, hires a – excuse the expression – actress, in what seems like an ill-conceived plot to get back at Jean. His plan being that he's going to kidnap Johnny Mac. How'm I doing?'

'Giving me the shivers,' I admitted.

'So this so-called genius with the ill-conceived plot winds up kidnapping the wrong kid and tries to convince the – excuse the expression – actress he hired that the kidnapped boy is all part of a movie plot. Did I actually hear the girl say she thought the kid was "method acting"?' Emmett asked.

'She said it to my face,' I admitted.

Emmett shook his head. Then went on, 'But she finally wises up and our so-called genius ties up both the girl and the little boy and sits around with his thumb up his ass. Why?'

'Waiting for instructions?' I suggested.

'My point exactly,' Emmett said.

'Well, we already figured there had to be someone else in on this, Emmett. The man is dead, after all, and it certainly wasn't natural causes, and if it was suicide, he *was* a genius, at least at hiding the gun.'

'No, now, Milt, we figured there was someone else in on it, sure. But didn't you think it was a subordinate? Someone working *for* Hawthorne?'

I thought about it. 'See your point,' I said. 'Maybe it was the other way around. Now Hawthorne was the one with revenge on his mind, but maybe the other person had other ideas. Ransom?'

'Blackmail?' Emmett suggested.

I shrugged my ignorance. 'You have Anthony check Motel Five and the Longbranch Inn? Make sure we don't have any strangers in town?'

'Done,' Emmett said. 'Holly Humphries is the only one staying at the Longbranch, and the Motel Five has a salesman that stops there regularly on his route, and an older couple on their way to Missouri to see their daughter and her kids.'

'Don't know how the Motel Five stays in business,' I said.

'You ever seen it on a Friday night? After the football game? I think they're surviving on by-the-hour bookings.'

'School board know about that?' I asked.

'I dunno, Milt. Would you rather 'em doing it on a nice soft bed in an enclosed room, or in the back seat of a car out on some lonely stretch of road?'

'Hey, the back seat of a car was good enough for me—' I started.

Emmett laughed. 'Yeah, but you had that fifty-five Chevy. You ever do it in a Toyota? How about a Mini Cooper?'

We had a good laugh at that image, all the while both of us, I'm sure, wondering where to go next on the murder of Emil Hawthorne.

FOURTEEN

JEAN

Since his retirement ten years earlier, Jean MacDonnell's father, Ben, had been bored beyond belief. When Jean called with the puzzle of finding out the whereabouts of a nun formerly known as Greta Schwartzmann Nichols, he didn't waste any time. It took him less than two hours to accomplish his task.

Jean was with a patient when her dad called back, but as soon as the patient left, DeSandra ran into Jean's office. 'Your father called!' DeSandra said, all excited. 'He said for you to call him back immediately! Is everything OK? Is your mother sick? Oh, God, I hope it's not one of your siblings! My sister, the one two up from me – not the one I'm real close to who's one down from me – anyway, she had her appendix rupture while she was at the KMart and she almost died! This was like two years ago, and nobody in my family has been to the KMart since then—'

'Thanks, DeSandra,' Jean said. 'I need to return his call—'

'Well, let me know if your mom's OK!' DeSandra said.

'I will,' Jean replied, getting up and helping DeSandra out of her office, then closing the door behind her.

Once back at her desk with the door safely closed, she called her father on his cell phone, as the note instructed. When he picked up, she could tell by the clatter of glassware and the calls of 'Jack and seven!' and 'Royal on ice!' that her father was at the country club's Nineteenth Hole.

'Daddy? You found something for me?' she asked.

'Sure did, baby,' he said. 'I was playing with Ted this morning anyway,' (the Archbishop of the Chicago Diocese) 'and he just made a call to somebody who looked it up. Anyway, your girl Greta is now Sister Mary Mark and she's an internist at Our Lady of Perpetual Sorrows Medical Center in Cleveland. Here's the number,' he said and rattled if off.

Jean thanked her father profusely and hung up, then dialed the Cleveland number. She had to leave a message for Sister Mary Mark, but then she only had to wait less than half an hour. She'd told DeSandra that she needed to be interrupted if the call came in. She was with a patient, a truck driver who was having trouble juggling his wife, his career and two out-of-town girlfriends, when DeSandra knocked and came into Jean's office.

'I'm sorry, Doctor, but that phone call you were expecting . . .'

'Thank you, DeSandra,' Jean said. Then she turned to the truck driver and said, 'If you'll excuse me for just a minute. I'll add the time at the end of your session,' then she left for DeSandra's desk outside her office.

Jean picked up the phone. 'Jean MacDonnell.'

'Dr MacDonnell? This is Sister Mary Mark at Our Lady of Perpetual Sorrows Medical Center in Cleveland, Ohio. I had a message here to call you,' the voice said, with a mild German accent.

'Yes, Sister Mary Mark, thank you so much for returning my call,' Jean said. 'I'm afraid this is a rather personal call and might be uncomfortable for you, so if you're not somewhere you can talk comfortably, I can call you back—'

'I'm fine, Dr MacDonnell. What is this about?'

'Emil Hawthorne,' Jean said. There was an immediate silence on the other end of the line. Finally, Jean said, 'Sister Mary Mark? Greta? Are you there?'

'That's a name I haven't heard in a very long time,' the nun finally answered. 'Either Emil Hawthorne *or* Greta.'

'Were you aware of Emil's coma?' Jean asked.

'Yes,' Sister Mary Mark said. 'I prayed for him daily.'

'Well, your prayers worked, Sister. He came out of the coma about eight or nine months ago.'

'Praise God,' the former Greta Schwartzmann Nichols said, so sotto-voiced that Jean had to question the sincerity of those prayers.

'Unfortunately, he was shot and killed yesterday,' Jean said.

'I'll pray for his soul,' Sister Mary Mark said with the same inflection she'd used to praise God for Emil's recovery.

Taking a deep breath, Jean plunged in. 'May I ask where you were yesterday, Sister?'

'Here,' Sister Mary Mark answered. 'Why do you ask?'

'I know there were some . . . bad feelings . . . between you and Emil Hawthorne,' Jean said, treading carefully. 'We're looking at anyone who might have had a motive . . .'

There was a laugh from the other end of the line. 'You think I killed Dr Hawthorne? Dear Lord!' she said, and laughed again. 'It's true that at one time in my life I hated him, but since finding God, I've replaced all hate with love. I'll admit it's been very hard to love Emil Hawthorne, but I've tried very hard to do that. I can't say it won't be easier to pray for his soul, though, rather than his living, breathing body.'

'You mean you're glad he's dead?' Jean interpreted.

'I mean, I'm glad, since he's out of his coma, that he can't hurt people anymore.'

'Did he hurt you?' Jean asked.

'Isn't that why you're calling?' Sister Mary Mark asked.

'I know Emil Hawthorne had a bad habit of seducing his interns,' Jean said.

'Yes, he did,' Sister Mary Mark replied.

'And that you were one of those,' Jean said.

Sister Mary Mark was silent for a long moment. Then she said, 'It wasn't my finest hour.'

'I saw you, the semester after you were his intern,' Jean said. 'The two of you were arguing in his office. The blinds were open. You seemed to be pleading with him.'

'I could say I don't remember the incident; that could be true. But it isn't. I remember it precisely. It was the turning point of my life. I came to him because I was pregnant, and I thought he would do the right thing.' Sister Mary Mark laughed. 'He wasn't even that shocked. More disgusted than anything else. He actually reached in his pocket and brought out his checkbook and asked me how much.' She let out what sounded somewhat like a laugh. 'I was crushed. I confess that I thought about suicide. God punished those thoughts by giving me a stillborn child,' the nun said.

The psychiatrist in Jean wanted to leap into the fray, console this wounded woman, let her know that God didn't work like that. But would a woman who'd chosen a life with God over a life with a husband and children believe or even care what Jean said? Could this wounded bird have made a life outside the rarified air of the Church?

'I'm so sorry,' was all Jean said.

'As am I,' said Sister Mary Mark.

'Do you know of any other women—'

Sister Mary Mark laughed. 'Oh my goodness, yes. Any other women involved with Emil? Half the staff at the hospital and definitely any intern who worked closely with him. There was a rumor about a woman the year before me. I never met her, but it seems Emil got taken by her, which I can only assume very rarely happened. If ever. One of the nurses said he was actually in love.' Sister Mary Mark sighed. 'Although I doubt seriously Emil had the capacity to love. Lust, though, is another matter entirely.'

'Do you know who the woman was?' Jean asked.

'Dr Johnson is all the nurse said. I don't remember hearing her first name.'

'Well, thank you, Sister. You've been a big help. And if

you ever want to talk about what happened to you with Emil—'

'I have God for that, Dr MacDonnell. Good day,' the nun said and hung up.

Jean went back into her office and finished her session with the truck driver, giving him the extra minutes the phone call had taken from his session. He was the last patient of the day, so she went immediately to her computer and back to the graduating classes at her alma mater. Assuming 'Dr Johnson' would have graduated one to two years before – if she had attended the same medical school and hadn't transferred her internship from another school – she checked the years before her class. Looking at both years, there were four Johnsons. Only one was a woman. Annie Johnson.

Jean turned off her computer and headed to pick up her son.

HOLLY

Dalton drove Holly to the ritzy part of the county, the township of Bishop, explaining that this was where the sheriff's sister lived, as she was married to a man who owned eight car parts yards in their part of Oklahoma and was a very rich man indeed.

'But he's real down to earth,' Dalton told her. 'Just a regular guy. And the sheriff's sister and her kids are real nice, too.'

'That's nice,' Holly said absently as she looked at the huge houses in Bishop. The newer subdivisions had semi-mansions with half-acre plots and yard signs saying they were protected by this or that security company. Coming closer into town, the old streets boasted beautifully refurbished faux Victorian and Georgian homes, some private homes, some law offices or tax offices or real estate offices.

It was all fine and dandy until they hit the downtown area with its quaint boutiques and specialty shops, tearooms and theater.

Theater? Holly sat up and took notice. Right there on Main Street! The Main Street Playhouse! Live productions.

Open auditions in two weeks, the sign said. *Open auditions!* The theater! Where she really belonged!

'Stop!' she yelled at Dalton. Dalton slammed on his brakes.

'Huh?'

Holly jumped out of the car and ran up to the box office that was currently closed. But there were playbills and ads for past and future productions, as well as numbers to call for auditions. At first, she just stared, absorbing it all.

'Gosh, I wish I could go in there!' she breathed.

'Well, sure, if you wanna,' Dalton said.

Holly turned toward him quickly. 'You can get me inside?'

Dalton pulled at a retractable metal chain from his pocket on the end of which dangled more keys than Holly wanted to count. Each one was labeled, though, and Dalton found the right one, inserted it and they walked inside.

The building had originally been an old movie house, and the lobby reflected that. Old linoleum covered the floor and at the back of the lobby was a bar behind which was a popcorn machine and soda fountain. Glass cases full of Jujubes, Butterfingers, malted milk balls and other chocolatey delights were below the bar.

New dark red velvet curtains separated the lobby from the theater. Inside, it was dim until Dalton flipped a switch, bringing on the house lights. New red carpet with an abstract design covered the two aisles that separated the theater in to three sections: two small side sections and one large section in the middle. The walls of the theater were made up of a three-dimensional village scene, with lights glowing in the little shops and thatched-roof homes. There was a balcony hanging over the back half of the theater, with ornate, polished brass railings to keep people from falling over.

Up on the stage, Holly noticed that the screen was still there. She found the steps that led up to the stage and bounded up them.

'They play some old movies in the summertime,' Dalton explained, following her on to the stage, 'and they did this one play one time and used the screen to show backdrops. It was kinda cool.'

'How many plays a year do they do?' Holly asked, a little breathless.

'About four or five, I think,' Dalton answered.

'Do they pay the actors?' she asked.

Dalton shrugged. 'I dunno.'

'Probably not,' Holly said, mostly to herself. 'I'll have to get a job somewhere. But I can do it. I can.'

'Do what?' Dalton asked.

'Become a star,' she said softly, standing on the stage and looking out at the 100-seat audience that wasn't there – yet.

MILT

I was headed home on Highway-5 when my cell phone rang.

'Sheriff Kovak,' I said, in my serious sheriff voice.

'Sheriff, this is Mindy at John's day care—'

'The hospital?' I asked.

'No, Sir, this is his morning day care. Rosie's Garden?'

'Yeah, Mindy, what can I do for you?' I asked.

'Well, Sir, I've been trying to call Dr MacDonnell, but she's not answering at either number,' Mindy said.

'What's the problem? Johnny Mac get in trouble today?' We'd been working on his behavior but he wasn't what you'd call consistent.

'No, Sir, it's not that. The deal we have is John is here half days and goes to the hospital day care at noon when Dr MacDonnell picks him up. They go to McDonald's most days—'

'Yeah?' I said. I knew this. The hard way, remembering Friday's fiasco.

'She didn't pick him up today, and it's almost our normal closing time, and I still can't get hold of her . . .'

My stomach turned over and I thought I was gonna throw up, except I don't do that. Throw up. I did a 180 on the highway, pissing off a few people, then put the bubble light on the roof of the Jeep and headed back into town at the Jeep's top speed. I needed a tune-up so the top speed at this point was only around ninety.

'Tell Johnny Mac I'm on my way,' I said and hung up.
I used my CPB radio to call the office and got Emmett.
'Jean never picked up Johnny Mac at noon,' I said. 'Go to
the hospital; see if you can find her. Get Anthony to put an
APB out on Jean's car. I'll get Johnny Mac and take him
to Jewell Anne's. I'll call you when that's done.'

'What the fuck, Milt?' Emmett said.

'Yeah,' I said and clicked off the radio. Pushing the Jeep
up to ninety-five.

EMMETT

Emmett took a squad car, lights and sirens blazing, and
headed the five miles to the county hospital where Jean
worked in the afternoons. He stopped the car smack-dab
in front of the main door and ran inside, immediately
finding security guards on their way to tell him to move
his car.

He flashed his badge and said, 'Do a lock down and start
searching every nook and cranny for Dr Jean MacDonnell.
Five foot ten, brown on brown, leg braces and crutches.'

'Yeah, we know Dr MacDonnell. Good woman,' said one
of the older guards.

'Then find her,' Emmett said and raced to the elevator
for the fifth floor and Jean's office.

Since Jean worked on the psych ward, there was a locked
door right in front of the elevators. It took Emmett precious
minutes to get someone to answer his knocks and yells.
Finally, an orderly, an African-American man in his mid-
fifties, wearing the white scrubs that signify the psych ward,
came up to the gate.

'What?' he said, his tone belligerent.

Emmett showed his badge. 'Let me in,' he said, his tone
brooking no argument.

'Under whose authority, Deputy?' the orderly said. 'We
don't just let somebody in here 'cause they show a badge.'

'Is Dr MacDonnell here?' Emmett said.

'Ha! That ain't gonna do you no good! Dr MacDonnell
hasn't been here all day.'

'You sure about that?' Emmett persisted.

'Yes, I'm sure! Do I look like somebody who ain't sure? I'm doing a fuckin' double today so I know the woman ain't been here all day, 'cause we had a reason to want her to be here around three this afternoon, and I paged my finger to the nub and she never answered, now did she?'

Without answering, Emmett hit the elevator button, and when the car didn't come immediately, he spied the exit sign by the stairs and ran down them.

MILT

Johnny Mac was waiting for me in the front room of his day care. It was after six in the evening and the Mindy who had called said, 'I'm so sorry, Sheriff, but I'm going to have to charge you extra for today. Not only do I have to charge you for the afternoon, when he normally isn't here, but we close at six and there is a severe penalty for not picking your children up by six. A dollar a minute. And it's . . .' She looked at the clock and tried to do the math.

I had a twenty in my pocket. I threw it on the desk. 'We'll settle up what we owe you later,' I said, and picked up my son in my arms. It was pretty apparent that my boy had been crying, and my heart was breaking for him, sitting there for hours, waiting for a mother who didn't show. And the thought of that turned my heart to ice, wondering why. Why didn't Jean show up to pick up our son? The only reason I could think of was something bad had happened. A wreck. An assault.

I tried to put that out of my mind to reassure my son, got him in his car seat and headed to Bishop, using my cell phone to call my sister, Jewell Anne, to let her know as much as I could with Johnny Mac sitting in the back seat listening to every word.

My sister was standing in her driveway when we drove up. Jewell Anne and me hadn't been close growing up as I was some thirteen years older than her, but trouble brings a family together and she had her share of it in Houston with her first husband. She and her kids lived with me for a while after that, until Jewell Anne's first love, a guy I helped my daddy get rid of 100 years ago, came back in to her life. He proved my daddy wrong, too. Daddy said the boy would come to no good; instead he now owns half of Oklahoma – at least the wrecked car part of it.

Jewell Anne had the back door open and Johnny Mac in her arms before I'd come to a complete stop. 'Go!' she said, waving me on. And go I did.

JEAN

It was getting on toward noon and Jean headed to the parking lot of her new office building to go get her son John and have their lunch. Her mind was on a patient recently admitted to the psych ward at the hospital. The meds she'd ordered weren't working, one of her interns had told her, and she needed to meet with the patient as soon as she got John settled. The woman had tried to kill her child, a two-year-old, which worried Jean. Two years is a long time for postpartum psychosis; she was betting on a more long-standing problem that had been showing itself in ways her family hadn't seen until now.

Her hand was on the door handle of her car when she heard her name called. She turned to see her partner heading toward her.

'Hey, Anne Louise,' Jean said, smiling. 'What's up?'

'Are you headed for the hospital?' Anne Louise Cursey asked.

'Eventually. I have to pick up John first for lunch.'

'Oh,' Anne Louise said, obviously disappointed.

'Is something up?' Jean asked. 'I can call Milt and have him go get John.'

'No, I don't want you bothering Milt about this. Could you just give me a ride? Where is John's morning day care?'

Jean laughed. 'About half a mile from the McDonald's. It's a conspiracy.'

'As far as the McDonald's would be fine,' Anne Louise said, getting in the shotgun side of the car.

Jean shrugged, opened the back door, laid her crutches across John's car seat and got behind the wheel.

DALTON

Dalton got the call on his radio as he and Holly were leaving Bishop.

'Car Three,' Dalton said.

'Hey, Dalton, it's Anthony. Get to the shop pronto. Bad stuff going down.'

'Ah, I got Miz Humphries in the car with me. Should I drop her off at the Longbranch?'

'What's your twenty?' Anthony asked.

'About ten miles from Longbranch coming out of Bishop,' Dalton said.

'No time for the Longbranch. Bring her with you. Out.'

'Ten-four, over and out,' Dalton said, one of the rare members of Milt's department to actually use the codes.

'What's going on?' Holly asked.

Dalton shook his head but put on his lights and sirens. 'Don't know. Guess we'll find out soon enough.'

They got to the office in less than ten minutes, pulling up to the side entrance and baling out. Once inside, they found Anthony, Emmett, Gladys, Lonnie Sturgis and Jasmine Bodine Hopkins, who was supposed to be on maternity leave, all on the phones or milling about looking anxious.

'Gladys, what's up?' Dalton asked, going up to her place at the desk where she was holding Jasmine and Emmett's baby girl, tears running down her face.

'Jean's missing!' she said. 'Johnny Mac was sitting at the morning day care all day waiting for her! Why that stupid woman at the day care didn't call Milt sooner, I'll never know. But she's going to get a piece of my mind, I can guarantee you that!'

'Where's Milt?' Dalton asked.

'Taking Johnny Mac to Jewell Anne's house . . . Oh, I just don't know what to do!' Gladys said, beginning to cry in earnest.

Holly saw that the only other woman in the room, apparently the mother of the baby, was on the computer, typing like crazy, so she held out her hands to Gladys.

'Let me take the baby for you, Miss Gladys,' Holly said.

Gladys handed over the baby. She was a tiny thing, maybe a month old at the most, and Dalton noticed how carefully Holly held her, hand behind her neck, as she walked her over to one of the orange chairs and sat down, cradling the baby in her arms. He had to tear himself away from the sight; he needed to do his job.

'Her car's not in the lot at her office building or the hospital parking lot,' Emmett said, coming up to Dalton. 'Get in your car and drive, Dalton. Find her.'

'Yes, Sir,' Dalton said, and, with one last look at Holly and the baby, headed out the side door for his car, Anthony following to head out in his.

FIFTEEN

MILT

It was the hardest thing I've ever done, leaving Johnny Mac with Jewell Anne, telling him I was going to pick up Mommy, telling him I'd be back in just a little while, waving and smiling as I drove off. Lying out of my ass to my four-year-old son.

I was sick with fear. No way in hell this wasn't connected to the whole Emil Hawthorne fiasco. Whoever had killed Emil Hawthorne had my wife. I was as sure of that as I was that the sun would come up in the morning. But, on the other hand, if anything happened to Jean, there was a good chance the sun would never come up again – at least not for me.

I headed straight for Jean's office. I doubted either Anne Louise or DeSandra would be there this late. It was after seven now. Which meant Jean had been missing for over six hours. As I pulled the car up to the entrance of Jean's building, I opened my door and leaned out, puking for the first time in my memory.

I wiped my mouth with my handkerchief, stepped over the mess I'd made and found the key Jean had given me for the door to the building. There was another one for the door to her office, which was on the third floor. I used that to get in.

The office was dark. I turned on the lights and headed for Jean's private office. Flipping through her Rolodex, I found the phone numbers for both Anne Louise and DeSandra. Neither answered their home numbers, so I left messages for both. Then, finding their cell phone numbers, I dialed those, too. No answer to either of those.

I sat down at Jean's desk and turned on her computer. I knew her password just like she knew mine. I put in Johnmac, then checked out her last action. She'd been looking at her medical school graduation roster, except not hers, but the one from the year before. I moved some papers around on her desk, and found the following:

Eric Loeman – Houston, MD
GSN = Sister Mary Mark
Johnson – EH in love?
Annie! Bingo!!

I knew about Eric Loeman, the oncologist at MD Anderson hospital who'd told her that Greta Schwartzmann Nichols had joined a convent. Obviously her nun's name was Sister Mary Mark. But where she was located wasn't in Jean's note. 'Johnson – EH in love?' 'EH'? Emil Hawthorne? But who was Johnson? Who was Annie? Hell, who was Bingo?

JEAN

Jean wasn't sure where she was. It was dark, smelled bad and was hot and stuffy. Trying to move, she realized she was tied up, both her hands and her feet. She thought tying her feet was serious overkill. Then she thought maybe she shouldn't be thinking about words like 'overkill'. Or any form of the word 'kill', come to think of it.

She tried kicking out with her legs, but her legs didn't have the strength to do much more than straighten themselves, which did hit the end of the box or whatever she was lying in, but not with what one might call gusto.

The lid to the box opened, and a voice came from a face silhouetted in the light behind her. It was a woman, and the voice sounded familiar. 'So you're awake.' She jerked Jean out by the arm, standing her up in the box. At that point, Jean saw her captor perfectly.

'What's going on, Anne Louise?' she asked her partner.

DESANDRA LOGAN

DeSandra had seen Anne Louise get in the car with Jean. Whatever was going down, it was going down tonight. She called for backup and followed the two women. When Jean MacDonnell's car pulled off Highway-5, going up the road that led to that quack doctor's crime scene, DeSandra kept on Highway-5, knowing that following Jean's car up that hill would be a dead giveaway. She called in her new location to her backup, asking for no lights or sirens.

Five miles down the road, DeSandra braked and did a 180, heading back to the side road up Mountain Falls. She cut her lights as she turned up the road, slowing to five miles an hour as she eased up on the old cotton farm with the barn where the quack had met his maker.

This was surprising to DeSandra. Drugs, sure – but murder? She had no idea that crazy stalker doctor had been in on Anne Louise and Jean's scam. She parked her car by the broken down barbed wire fence that used to contain the cotton field, got out and walked toward the barn, staying in the shadows of the trees that lined the old driveway.

She knew she should wait for backup, but that wasn't in DeSandra's nature. DeSandra Logan was a cowboy, a rogue, a renegade. DeSandra Logan was a lone wolf. She didn't need no stinking backup!

MILT

I left Jean's office and headed to Anne Louise's house. She lived in Bishop, which was going back the way I'd come when I'd dropped off Johnny Mac, but it wasn't to be helped. Maybe the two women were there, just not answering the phone. Someone could have them trapped in the house – like that crazy secretary of theirs, although I couldn't think why.

I'd been able to decipher Jean's notes and the last page she'd looked at on her computer. I knew enough to realize that Jean was looking for someone named Annie Bingo Johnson. Why, I didn't know, and I wasn't sure how to find out, short of calling my in-laws to see if they knew a way of finding out where Sister Mary Mark, the former Greta Schwartzmann Nichols, was. That seemed to be the direction the information had flowed. But I wasn't up to talking to either of them at the moment. I didn't want to tell them that I had no idea where my wife – their daughter – might be, and, oh yeah, Dad, there's a killer on the loose.

HOLLY

Holly watched all the activity around her as the deputies rushed in and out of the station. Telephones rang and Gladys, wiping tears from her eyes, would answer them like a professional and, as soon as she hung up, burst into tears again. Jasmine, mother of the baby Holly was holding, kept up a steady stream of typing on the computer, running to the fax machine, the printer and back to the computer.

Holly had changed little Lily Marie's diaper, fed her a bottle of expressed milk her mother had stuck in the sheriff department's kitchen refrigerator and had just rocked her to sleep, swaying the baby back and forth in her arms. There was a mesh-screened travel bed set up next to Jasmine's desk, and Holly very carefully placed Lily Marie in it. Jasmine was on the phone and the computer simultaneously, but managed to smile her thanks to Holly. Holly smiled back, gave a little finger wave, and headed back over to the orange chairs, wishing there was something she could do to help.

She liked Jean a lot. She'd been a big help to Holly when she was first brought in here, and she hoped she'd be able to return the favor real soon.

The front door burst open and Dalton came in. Seeing Holly, he went over to the orange chair section first.

'Hey,' he said, smiling tentatively. 'You doing OK?'

'Just got Lily to sleep,' she said, smiling back. 'What can I do to help?'

'You know how to make coffee?' Emmett asked, over-hearing their conversation.

Holly stood up. 'Yes, Sir. I sure do.'

Emmet nodded his head toward the kitchen and, with a backward glance and smile at Dalton, Holly went to make coffee.

After the coffee was made, Holly went back out to the big room. Gladys was at the fax machine, Jasmine was on the computer and Dalton and Emmett, the only others left at the station, were conferring over a map of the county. The phone began to ring. Looking around, and seeing no one running toward it, Holly picked it up.

'Prophesy County Sheriff's Department,' she said.

'Who the hell is this?' came a voice Holly immediately recognized.

'It's me, Holly, Sheriff,' she said. 'Everybody was busy so I—'

'Let me talk to Emmett,' the sheriff said.

Holly found the hold button and called out to Emmett. 'Emmett, Sheriff's on line one.'

He nodded and headed to the phone nearest him.

The main line rang again. Holly picked it up. 'Prophesy County Sheriff's Department. How may I direct your call?'

JEAN

She was in the barn where she was sure Emil Hawthorne had died. She could see the yellow crime scene tape around the space where the barn doors had once been. Milt's people and the medical examiner's people were finished here. Any other business they had could wait until morning, and

morning was a long ways away. Jean had her doubts of
whether she'd make it that long, what with the gun her
partner had pointed at her face.

'Sit down on that hay bale!' Anne Louise said, pushing
Jean. Jean didn't have her crutches and she fell, the top
half of her landing on the bale, but her bottom half landing
on the dirt floor of the barn. Anne Louise laughed. 'Jesus,
you're pathetic!' she said. She jerked Jean up by her arm,
getting her into a sitting position.

'Why couldn't you just leave it alone?' Anne Louise
asked. 'I had everything under control! I should have known,
after what you did to Emil back in Chicago, that I couldn't
trust you to leave anything alone!'

'Anne Louise,' Jean said, keeping her voice even, 'I don't
understand.'

'Oh, for God's sake, Jean, don't try playing shrink with
me! I'm better at it than you've ever been!'

'Annie,' Jean said. She looked up at her partner. 'Is your
maiden name Johnson?'

Anne Louise laughed. 'Oh you are just so smart, aren't
you, you big old gimp? Yes, I went by Annie for a while
as an intern. I got tired of Anne Louise after medical school.
But Annie's kind of a silly name. Not the name of an MD,
know what I mean? Had to go back to Anne Louise and
then I married the asshole and got stuck with Cursey.
Noticed you didn't change your name when you married
your hick.'

'I already had a career established as MacDonnell,' Jean
said.

'And what a career, too, huh, Jeannie the crip? Head
honcho at this stupid podunk hospital in the middle of
fucking Oklahoma, of all places!' Anne Louise said.

'Then why did you come here?' Jean asked. 'Why did
you want to be my partner?'

'Chicago was getting a little too hot to handle,' Anne Louise
said. 'There are things people just don't understand . . .'

'Like a multimillion-dollar practice supported by the sale
of Oxycodone?' came a voice from the open barn door.

Anne Louise swung around with her gun and fired at

DeSandra Logan, who fired back. Jean fell over backwards, using the hay bale as a shield.

MILT

Milt had checked out Anne Louise's house. No lights, no answer at the front or back door. Everything locked up tight. He had no idea where DeSandra lived, but he called her home and cell phone numbers again. She picked up on the second ring of her cell phone.

'Mike! That you? Where the hell are you guys?' she said, her voice loud. Milt heard the crack of a gunfire.

'DeSandra?' he shouted into the phone. 'What the hell's going on? This is the sheriff!'

'Milt? Where the hell's my backup?' DeSandra screamed.

'What backup? What are you talking about? Who's shooting?'

Another shot rang out and DeSandra screamed. 'The . . . barn,' she said, her voice haggard. 'The barn!'

Milt figured she must have dropped the phone, because he could still hear background noises, but not DeSandra. 'DeSandra?' he shouted into the phone. 'DeSandra?'

There was no answer and he disconnected the call, picking up his police ban radio. '911!' he shouted into the radio.

'Hello?' came the voice he knew to be Holly's. Unfortunately, she didn't know how to work the radio and didn't release the button so he could talk. Finally, Emmett's voice came over the radio. 'Milt?'

'Something's going down at the barn! I know DeSandra Logan's been shot! Jean's gotta be there! I'm on my way. Get your asses over there!' Milt said and turned off his radio. He didn't need the chatter. He just needed his bubble top light and a heavy foot on the accelerator.

JEAN

'Sweet Jesus, you killed her!' Jean said, looking at DeSandra's body lying in the open doorway of the barn.

'Goddamn! Who would think that stupid woman was

DEA?' Anne Louise said as she walked up to DeSandra's body. She attempted to kick her in the ribs, but DeSandra grabbed her leg and pulled Anne Louise to the ground.

Anne Louise still held the gun in her hand. DeSandra grabbed her wrist, trying to wrestle the gun away from her, or at least to move it away from her own body. DeSandra stuck a long fingernail in Anne Louise's wrist, numbing her hand and letting the gun drop to the ground. Anne Louise jumped up, heading for the gun.

Jean lifted herself up from the bale of hay, using a farm machine of some sort to help her stand. She wasn't sure where her crutches were, probably still in the car that was outside of the barn. Holding onto the one piece of machinery, she worked her way to a chain hanging from the ceiling. She pulled on it to see if it would hold her weight; instead, the entire chain came down in her hands. It wasn't a particularly long or heavy chain, but she thought it might do the trick.

Jean swung the chain around her head, letting it gather momentum, then let it go. The chain hit Anne Louise in the head and she dropped like a sack of rocks.

MILT

I tore up the side road on Mountain Falls, then down the driveway to the barn. My wife was on the ground, DeSandra Logan resting with her head in Jean's lap.

'Hey,' Jean said smiling as I walked up. 'You're late. I've already called an ambulance. But go look what I did.' She nodded her head back into the barn and I went in to find Anne Louise Cursey out cold, with a heavy metal chain wrapped halfway around her neck.

I walked back out to where Jean sat on the ground with DeSandra. 'Logan, you OK?' I asked.

'Two shots, one to my shoulder, the other a through-and-through on the side. Might have taken a rib with it,' she said.

All of a sudden we heard sirens screaming up the side road to the barn's driveway. The first two cars on the scene were my guys and an ambulance; the next four turned out to be DeSandra's backup.

Jumping out of a still moving car, a young African-American man, dressed in blue jeans and a DEA windbreaker, ran up to DeSandra.

'Babe, you OK?' he said, kneeling down and pushing DeSandra's hair out of her face.

She hit him with an open hand. 'What the hell took you so long, Mike? I had to get saved by a damned shrink!' she said.

'We lost your GPS signal,' Mike said. 'We had to go to the sheriff's office. We were just damned lucky they were already getting in their unit to come here. We just followed.'

DeSandra shook her head. 'Jesus. As usual. The DEA – a day late and a dollar short.'

CHARLIE

Charlie heard the commotion on the radio. He called Milt on his cell, asked if he needed backup. A very happy Milt Kovak reported that no, he didn't – all was well.

'Great,' Charlie said. 'Just a heads up, though, Milt. You know that ammonia/bleach case? Boy, we gotta talk.'

EPILOGUE

MILT

Anne Louise Johnson Cursey had a very sore neck. She was seen in the emergency room while handcuffed to a gurney. The next gurney over was occupied by DeSandra Logan, but not for long. They took her up to surgery, an anxious DEA agent named Mike following beside her, holding her hand.

My wife was seen, too. She had scratches and bruises, and her paralyzed legs had taken a beating. She had a broken anklebone on the left and a dislocated knee on the right.

It took me a couple of days to get all the info and figure out what the hell had been going on. Old Emil Hawthorne was doing just what we thought he was doing: going after Jean for vengeance, plain and simple. He felt she'd ruined his life, and he decided to ruin hers.

But he'd needed more help than just that of Holly Humphries, wannabe actress. Emil had gone looking for his old flame – the only real love of his life – Anne Louise Cursey, the former Annie Johnson. Not only had they been lovers when she was his intern, but he had actually helped her start her side business, which was used to pay her way through internship and residency, pay for a beautiful wedding (after Emil was out of her hair and in a coma), buy a very nice house in mid-town Chicago, pay for the best schools for her son and buy some fairly decent jewelry for herself. Her husband had belonged to the best country club and their vacations had been to places like Venice, Tahiti and Greece.

The other Dr Cursey, Anne Louise's ex-husband, Ted, a dermatologist, had just assumed his wife's psychiatric practice was booming a little more than it actually was.

By the time Anne Louise ran into Jean at the convention

in Las Vegas, she had already divorced a very confused
Ted, who couldn't understand why there wasn't more money
in the accounts of her private practice.

Anne Louise had never really changed her sideline, it
was just too lucrative, and nobody seemed to notice. As an
intern, she had a key to the drug closet and would take out
the class-C narcotics, replacing them with placebos. She
was very careful to take only a few out of each bottle, so
that the placebos wouldn't be noticed.

She was caught her second year as an intern. By Emil
Hawthorne. Who knew a guy, who knew a guy. And what
had been Anne Louise's little sideline became a very lucrative business, laundered through a rather pedestrian psychiatric
practice. By the time Emil Hawthorne went into his coma,
Anne Louise had all the connections she needed and was
rather happy to be rid of the fawning Emil.

The DEA became interested in Anne Louise almost a
year before Emil Hawthorne came out of his coma. They
just couldn't get any hard evidence and were unable to get
anyone into her operation.

As luck would have it, Anne Louise's marriage, practice
and side business all began to go south at about the same
time as the convention Jean and I went to in Las Vegas.
Anne Louise figured that laying low in 'Podunk', Oklahoma
would save her side business.

DeSandra Logan, who'd actually grown up in Bishop,
'came home' to take care of her mama, supposedly, and,
through some DEA shenanigans, was the only applicant for
the job of receptionist at the new psychiatric practice of
MacDonnell & Cursey. The DEA assumed that Jean was
in on the Oxycodone business.

For Emil Hawthorne, it was sheer luck that the love of his
life was in the same place as the person he blamed for all
his problems. At his insistence, he and Anne Louise started
up where they'd left off, and he enlisted her in his scheme
to get back at my wife. The threat of exposure was enough
to keep Anne Louise in line – at least until she shot him.

Charlie Smith and me had a long talk about the 'accidental'
death of Kevin Holcomb, and my jurisdiction's 'accidental'

death of what would have been, had he lived, Kevin's father-in-law, Albert Canfield. It didn't take a rocket scientist, thank God, to figure out this one. Both ladies backed up each other on the abuse each took from their husbands, which might have justified a gunshot to the gut in the middle of a beating, but both of these murders were so premeditated they were at the point of being diabolical.

Carolina had learned well from her mama. Having had enough, what with the broken arm, Carolina's mama came over and helped her set up the bathroom. She sealed the window with duct tape, poured ammonia in the tank of the toilet and bleach in the bowl, lit a strongly scented candle, and waited for her husband to go pee.

In a strange way, Carolina was luckier than her mama, who had to push her dresser up to the door and lean on it to keep her husband in. Carolina's husband had already put a bolt on the bathroom door. The master bathroom was Carolina's punishment for whenever Kevin got irritated with her. He locked her in there often, and for up to days at a time.

So when Kevin finally went to pee that evening, Carolina bolted the door, stuffed the crack beneath with a towel and waited for him to flush the toilet. When he did, the ammonia and bleach mixed, and there was no place for the gas to go, except into Kevin's lungs. He tried, of course, to get out of the bathroom, beating on the door to no avail. Carolina said she just sat on the bed and listened to him, and cried a lot. She really did love him, she said.

So Charlie Smith's got a trial coming up for murder one against Carolina Canfield Holcomb, and we got a similar trial coming up against her mama, Roberta Canfield.

A couple of days after we settled all the stuff with Anne Louise Cursey and Emil Hawthorne, Anthony Dobbins drove Dalton Pettigrew to Tulsa to pick up his car, which had been towed to police impound. There wasn't much left of it. It had been stripped of anything sellable, including the bumpers. Far as I know, he's still dealing with the insurance company.

There have been a few changes at the shop, too. Jasmine's back full time. Her mama's taking care of baby Lily and

I try to make sure she and Emmett aren't doing overtime at the same time. We're family-friendly around here. Oh, and the big news: Gladys retired. Seems all the kidnapping stuff was just too much for her and she decided she was too old to handle it. The crying jag that started when Jean got kidnapped took two days to quiet down, what with Jean's talking to her and writing her a prescription and all.

We got a replacement for her right away, though. Holly Humphries is our new civilian clerk, although she insisted on a uniform for her job. She doesn't have a Sam Browne or a gun or anything, but she wears her khakis real proud. After two weeks on the job and Dalton not asking her out, Holly took that one into her own hands. They've been seeing each other now for about a month and Jean told me she advised Holly, strictly during girl talk and not in any way therapy (so it was OK for her to tell me), that if she wanted anything more out of Dalton anytime soon, Holly was going to have to do the seducing. I hate to say it, but I think Jean called that one right on the money.

Meanwhile, Holly's volunteering at the Main Street Playhouse in Bishop, right now helping to make props and painting stage backdrops, but they promised to let her keep auditioning for parts in their plays until she got it right.

Dalton's sister Mary Ellen is doing real well after her thirty days in the hospital and getting just the right meds to deal with her bipolar disorder. All her kids are doing fine and her husband Rodney is trying real hard to help out with the housework and the kids.

Dalton's mama has taken an extended vacation with her sister Eunice in Mexia (pronounced Ma-hay-ya), Texas, leaving Dalton on his own for the first time in his life. I think this new development might improve Holly's chances of getting up close and personal with a certain deputy.

And me? Well, I got a new-found appreciation for my wife, my boy and, Lord forgive me, Dalton Pettigrew. Dalton may be the tortoise to everybody else's hare, but the boy gets the job done.